ILLUSIONS
THAT MAY

ILLUSIONS THAT MAY

COURT HIGH: BOOK TWO

EDEN O'NEILL

ILLUSIONS THAT MAY: Court High Book 2
Copyright © 2020 by Eden O'Neill

This book is a work of fiction and any resemblance to any person, living or dead, any place, events or occurrences, is purely coincidental and not intended by the author.

Cover Design by Ever After Cover Design
Editing by Judy's Proofreading & Straight on till Morningside

CHAPTER
ONE

December

I spent homecoming in a sheriff's office when most people spent theirs screwing in hotels or getting fucked up at after-parties. I spent my homecoming alone, or at least, it felt that way. Words flittered around me that night, words about both possibility and tragedy. They circulated around me like a cyclone of leaves and debris, but they weren't for me despite being about me and my family. I wasn't supposed to know what was really going on, sitting behind glass and sipping tea with more than an unsettled stomach. I emptied my stomach just earlier that night, my sister's pretty dress dirty from when I fell in the dirt and got vomit on it.

God...

Rosanna had brought me a change of clothes to the sheriff's office, as well as the tea. She'd been hell-bent on bringing me home, but I wasn't going anywhere.

None of us would before we could find out more about my sister.

Dad was there too, of course, either on his cell phone or

yelling at cops. He wanted to know what the fuck was going on and why some news story downstate was reporting my sister's death when he'd just been called down to the sheriff's office about it. He wanted answers, and when he wasn't getting them quick enough, he called people. He called *his* people while I sat behind glass with Rosanna. She had her arm around me, cradling me with warmth, but that didn't matter. I was alone here.

I didn't even have Royal.

At homecoming, he, Jax, Knight, and LJ took me to the sheriff's office in urgency. Dad had actually sent Hubert to get me, bring me to the sheriff's office of Maywood Heights *alone*, and to be with family, but the boys weren't having that. Royal wasn't having that, and I wasn't either. He and the others wanted answers just as much as I did and they were family. They were my sister's family, blood or not. Royal held my hand the whole time, telling me it'd be okay. Telling me this *wasn't real* and it couldn't be. He'd heard from my sister. *He'd heard from her* and this was all just some fucked-up mistake and a viral news story. He couldn't be certain, though. None of us could, and the moment we arrived at the sheriff's office, Royal fired words at them. Seriously, he'd lost it, all the boys having to hold him back while he demanded the truth about my sister. Eventually, they separated him from me and my dad, the other boys going with him when the sheriff managed to calm the situation only by inviting Royal and the boys to come speak with him privately in his office. They could ask their questions, but they wouldn't be doing so in their current manner at the busy precinct.

"I'm going to figure this out," Royal'd said to me, his expression wrought with so many emotions. Tie undone and blond hair strewn, he had a horror behind his lustrous green eyes. He had a terror I hadn't wanted to see. It was different on him, foreign, and twisted my stomach even more than it already was.

Royal left after that, left with the sheriff and the rest of the boys, and I hadn't gotten to see him after that. He disappeared into the valley of cops and talk, and I myself was forced behind glass, the precinct's sitting room my place for the night. I was sheltered from everything while others talked around me. While Royal was gone, my dad was doing his own yelling, the man beet red with threats on his lips. In the past, he'd acted so cold about all things Paige, even me for a time, but all that obviously wasn't true. My dad cared. He didn't want his kid dead any more than anyone else would, and I saw that behind thick glass.

I saw that when the news hit.

What news my dad got exactly I didn't know, but he got something. He'd *heard* something before me and whatever it was made me stand up and go over to that glass. The cop he'd been speaking to had a walkie-talkie in his hands, the officer's face grave, and my dad's had bled of all color. He physically *paled* after the officer told him something.

I later found out it'd been the truth.

I lay in my bed hours later that night, alone again and tossing after a round of fresh tears. I drenched my pillowcase with them, Hershey in my arms and whining beside me. She didn't like when I was upset, my little Labrador puppy worried about me and she should be. She should worry. I was worried too as I was completely unable to determine how I would be able to get out of this bed after this very moment. My sister was gone, and my dad was too. He'd left, going downstate.

He had to identify my sister's body.

His words were still in my head, no longer behind thick glass when he finally came to speak to me. He'd erased his emotion then, maybe feeling like he had to? For me? I didn't know, but it was gone and that cold exterior returned. My hard-ass father was before me, telling me things and truths I didn't want to hear. He told me they had evidence. He told me they had facts about a girl who'd lost her life beneath a train. She'd been dragged, only recently discovered by a maintenance crew worker, and her story leaked the moment she'd been identified. The girl had a history with the law, underage drinking... minor stuff, but because of the things she'd gotten into, they had her fingerprints. They knew who she was. The only thing they had to do now was have family ID and claim the body, and I stopped listening after that, things about plane tickets and details regarding my dad's trip lost on me. I didn't want to hear this story about some girl who couldn't possibly be *my* sister. They made a mistake. Royal told me he'd heard from her.

He told me she was okay.

I refused to absorb any of it, currently on the cusp of a breakdown in my bed. For the umpteenth time, I attempted to text Royal for an update on whatever *he* was finding out, the truth. He'd have all the answers, and I knew he would. He cared about my sister. He cared about me, and I knew that's what he was trying to find out.

"I'm going to figure this out..."

A knock on my window made me drop my phone, and when I turned, a figure lingered outside on the second level. Broad and solid, a suited Royal Prinze hovered a hand to me, and I instantly rose from my bed. He didn't have to pull out his pocketknife this time to let himself into my life. He didn't have to do any of those things anymore.

Disheveled, Royal was down to his dress shirt and pants, his tux coat in his hand as he worked his way through my bedroom window. The pretty paper orchid on his tux was crushed, hanging from the jacket lapel and seemingly wilted. I'd done that, my body when he picked me up from the Windsor Preparatory Academy campus lawn. I hurled my guts out on that lawn, lost in a daze of emotions. He let me finish, but after, took me away. He told me Hubert was here to get me, but he and the guys were taking me away themselves.

We were all going to the sheriff's office, and my dad would meet us there.

So much of that was a blur, my life a movie on fast-forward, and nothing slowed down until this very moment. Royal was here. He was here *with the truth* and finally things would slow. He pulled me into his arms the moment he got feet to the floor, that mighty embrace so secure and filled with so much heat. Finally, things would be right. Finally, he'd give me something other than the bullshit I'd gotten.

"Dad's going downstate," I told him, not realizing I was crying until his dress shirt came away wet. I shook my head. "He had to go ID the body. But this is crazy. It's not Paige. You heard from her. You said she was okay. Did you show the cops? Show them your text messages from her? This is all a big mistake."

She told him that after an altercation with a girl she'd been seeing, she was going away. If my sister had been leaving like he said, all this other stuff wasn't true. Who they found couldn't have been her. The news had mentioned a girl being *dragged*, dragged south by a train, and there'd been whispers at the precinct that the train came from this area but that couldn't possibly be true. It couldn't be Paige. She was leaving town.

A finger rough and thick wiped away my tears, the blond silent as he watched me talk. I ignored the red in his eyes, the visible presence of anything but hope, because this was all a big mistake.

I talked again.

"You told them, right?" I asked him, *begged* him. "Told them the truth? It's not true what they're saying about Paige." This all was crazy and my dad would see that the moment he went south and saw whatever girl they had wasn't my sister. After that, he'd probably sue the fuck out of some people. The media obviously got on my sister's social media accounts, found her pictures. The ones the news had been showing all night came right from my sister's profiles. My jaw moved. "They're all going to pay for this. My sister isn't dead, and they're playing with my family."

Royal's hand came to cup my jaw, his expression morphing. It appeared more and more tragic the longer he wasn't *saying anything*.

"Royal..."

His gaze veered, eyes blinking. He dampened his lips. "It's her, Em," he said, the shortening of my name gutting me. His throat jumped. "Who they found was Paige."

"Stop it."

He held me steady when I tried to back up, held me firm. He gripped me. "I showed them the text messages, December. Showed them everything. Talked to the sheriff until I was blue in the face. They told me she sent them before. They told me..."

I shook, Royal bringing me close.

"They found alcohol in her system. Lots of it. There was evidence in a neighboring town. They think she wandered there via the tracks. They're saying it was an accident—"

"No. No. No!" I smacked at his chest, Royal wrestling with my hands. "You told me you heard from her. You told me she was fine!"

"She was, December. I swear to God. She was fine, and she had not one lick of alcohol that night. I know because..."

"Because what?"

He gripped me, his throat bobbing. "I was there. I was there, and I told you that. We were out on Route 80, but she didn't drink."

"Why were you guys out there? Why?"

He had to physically grab my hands now, his jaw working.

"That girl left her fucked up," he said, his swallow hard. "That girl she was seeing? Paige was angry, upset. She wanted to deal with it, but I was called away. My dad needed me that night for some stupid Court thing. I shouldn't have left. I should have stayed."

He said that, again and again. My face scrunched up. "How did she want to deal with it?"

He said nothing, his thumb moving along my jaw. "She wanted Court intervention, but I swear, December. She was fine. At least I thought she was. The drinking must have happened after I left somehow. I never gave her any alcohol. Didn't think she had anything, but she must have. The cops think she sent me the texts after she did attempt to leave, wandering the tracks to the next town, but she was drunk, December. Just so drunk." He paused, a gasp in his throat. "The time stamp on the texts were literally an hour before the train came through that town."

I dizzied then, dizzied until I fell into his arms. I hit at his biceps. I thrashed against them. I recalled my dad telling me something similar, that there was an accident and they found evidence my sister had been hit in a neighboring town, but how could I believe it? It contradicted *everything*.

Until it didn't.

It all came crashing down in a wave of reality, a wave I wasn't ready for and I wasn't the only one.

Mighty arms secured around me like a lifeline, like *I* was the lifeline and needed as equally as I needed the embrace. Royal buried his face into my neck, holding on to me for dear life.

"I'm so sorry, Em," he rasped, the words gasping over and over. He gripped my hair. "I'm so sorry."

He did nothing, *not* his fault. Paige'd wanted his help and he probably would have done anything to give that to her. He would have *ruined* the very existence of whoever this girl was who screwed over my sister. He just hadn't gotten the chance.

There were many times some of the things Royal did truly intimidated me and sometimes even scared me. He was intense and borderline lethal.

But he was also this.

He was caring, had a heart, and he showed me that with his vulnerability and comfort. He held me, consoling me when he himself no doubt was cut to ruins. I kissed him, his mouth pausing.

But then that stopped too, his hands coming down my shoulders until he had hands full of my bottom. I'd put on a T-shirt and bed shorts, and he pushed hands underneath the latter.

"December..." He kissed me hard, his mouth pulling apart my lips. He lifted me, my legs wrapped around his waist while he made me forget. He made us both forget, his hands pulling my ponytail holder out as he brought me to the bed. He set me down next to Hershey, kissing me.

"We shouldn't," he rasped, but didn't stop. He cradled my face. "We can't. I shouldn't..."

Maybe he didn't want to do this because of the situation. Maybe he knew we were both in pain, and clearly, this was an avenue to block any of that. But I knew something too. *I* needed him, and I know he needed me.

I pushed him back, only enough to place Hershey into her dog bed. After that, I was pulling him with me, guiding him to his back while I worked my clothes off. I tossed my T-shirt, my breasts free, and he cupped one, instantly making me cry out. I think it was too much because before I knew it, Royal shifted the tables.

He captured my lips, the entire mass of his hard body pinning me beneath him. Working off his shirt, he exposed his chest, golden and perfect and hot when he pressed himself against me. He thrust into me through my underwear, kissing me deep into the sheets.

"Em..." He quivered, actually quivering over me. "Em, I'm so sorry. I'm so damn sorry."

He kept saying that, that he was sorry. Sorry for me, us? I didn't know, but he was. He was sorry in this situation, and I was sorry too, sorry for us both. We shouldn't have to deal with this, but *this* is what we had, each other.

I tasted his tongue and he let me, his hand moving into my underwear. He touched me where it ached, and as I rose up, his eyes rolled back. Like he loved touching me just as much as I loved to be touched. He guided my legs out of my panties, and after working his pants down, he got a condom out of his wallet. He made sure that protection was on good between us. He protected *me*, and when he eased my legs apart, I cried out again.

"Royal..." I gripped his biceps, the tears falling. He kissed them away, shaking above me with every thrust. He moved slow at first, picking up and hugging me to him. He wouldn't let me go, apologizing again. He was really holding the burden and maybe forever since he'd been out there with my sister.

I cried while he apologized, the pair of us a complete mess, but we didn't stop. We didn't because it felt good. It felt close and loved, and I didn't think either one of us wanted to let go of that. We both knew what would happen once we were out of this bed and away from each other's arms. We did and we weren't ready.

Royal kissed me hard as I reached my peak, his thrusts hard as he hit his. Even still, he wouldn't let go. We both rode it out, tomorrow another day.

I hoped tomorrow never came.

CHAPTER
TWO

December

My sheets were free of Royal Prinze when I woke up, and it hurt how I'd become so dependent on him so quickly. When I first moved to Maywood Heights and came to Windsor Prep, I couldn't stand him and even borderline hated him.

So why now, did I shiver without his arms?

I grabbed my puppy instead, reaching down for her as the sun slammed harshly into my eyes. Between crying and whatever the hell time it was, my eyes weren't having it. My little chocolate lab hopped onto my bed the minute I leveled her with it, and I grabbed my phone after.

Royal: I had to leave and take care of something. I'm sorry.

Another one of his *sorry*s, fitting since I couldn't stop crying. Reality came back with a rush, and as I lay back down, my puppy licking my face, I could only close my eyes again. I couldn't do this day right now.

I just wasn't ready.

I think I fell asleep because by the time I woke up, the day was well into the afternoon. I knew by the fresh light that was no longer there and the chill around had me opening my eyes. My window let me see the impossible, snowflake flutters I'd only seen in pictures. It tended not to snow in California, but I guess in the Midwest, October was game. A knock hit my door behind me, and I said nothing, snuggling Hershey. Eventually, the door cracked open.

"December?"

I burrowed deeper into my blankets, knowing I was still naked from my night with Royal Prinze. I knew Rosanna was a girl, but I really wasn't trying to be seen naked on top of everything else. I lay quiet, and eventually, a step came into my room.

"Your dad's back," she said, a strain in her voice. I couldn't see her with my back turned but I didn't need to. I was sure she'd cried a few of her own tears, and though I didn't know how close she'd been with my sister, she'd been good to me. She'd been kind, and if our relationship was any indicator, she'd been the same with my sister. She'd been a friend too. Her sigh staggered. "He'd like to see you if you could come down."

My dad was back already. My dad was here with news.

I had to face reality again.

I had my puppy in my arms when I came downstairs, my oversize shirt and shorts on. After this talk with my dad, I had every intention of getting back into my bed and pulling the sheets over my head. I might even do that before the end of this talk if my strength didn't hold up. We would see, I guess.

Steps let my dad know I entered the room, his head moving. In his clothes from last night, he had his hands in his pockets, his back to me as he stared at the snowflakes I just discovered myself upstairs.

Rosanna led me to a seat, the woman's eyes just as red as

Royal's last night. She sat beside me on the couch, and squeezing Hershey, I put my legs up.

Dad angled his head back. "What did I say about having the dog on furniture?"

I stiffened, not expecting that. In the days leading up to this moment, my dad had certainly gotten better when it came to Hershey. He even let her live with us, the pink collar and tag around her neck even given to me by him. I fingered it. "I'll hold her. I promise."

His only response was a gaze out the window, and since he didn't protest about my proposal, I sat tight, stiff with a normally restless puppy. Was this how it would be with my dad again? We'd been making progress...

But that had been before, hadn't it? It'd been during a time when he finally started getting used to me being in his space and accepting my reasons for coming here. I came here for my sister. I hoped my presence would ultimately bring her back. She always came to rescue me, and knowing I was in her space, I thought she'd do the same. She'd always been very adamant about keeping me out of her world and her life here, and after living in it for a time, I understood. Besides the stuff going on with my father, there was a law here run by none other than Royal and other boys in town known as the Court. They were a pretty big fucking deal in this town, and I had crossed them a time or two. That'd been when I hadn't understood Royal and his relationship with Paige as his best friend. But when things had started to settle down on that front, the same ended up happened at home. My dad and I had started to get along, and dare I say, he wanted me here. I hadn't been a burden to him.

I breathed hard. "You saw her?" He came back so quickly. Had he even been gone?

My question went without words, my dad suddenly tense as he braced his arms. "I did. It was her... What was left anyway. There wasn't much."

A hand squeezed mine, Rosanna, and I closed my eyes, the tears squeezing down. No one could prepare themselves for something like this. I mean, what the fuck.

"And she was dragged, Mr. Lindquist?" Rosanna asked, braver than me. I had more questions too, but I refused to ask them.

My dad gave us that with his nod. "The officials are saying from Corrington Meadows, a town or so over. They're thinking she got hit sometime between four and six. A train went through during that time. It was dark, early in the morning."

It was dark.

Everything Royal said came flying back, everything true. Everything goddamn true.

"And the amount of alcohol the coroner said was in her system was off the charts," my dad explained, shaking his head. "She was out there, wandering around *wasted*, and got herself—"

"Dad?" I retched, an arm coming around and squeezing me. Rosanna rubbed my arm, my tears falling again. I didn't care what my sister did. He couldn't talk that way about her. Not now.

Dad closed his lips, his hands moving to slide inside his pockets. Turning away, he faced the window again. "I've chosen to have her cremated considering."

I closed my eyes again, not wanting to hear any of this. This was the point where I wanted to run from the conversation and back into my blankets. This was just too fucking much, but I stayed, holding on tight to my puppy.

"I guess all that's left now is to pack."

I lifted my head. "Pack?"

Dad nodded just once. "You'll be taking time out of school, and I've already notified them, as well as leave from your job. We're going to California. Your aunt already knows we're coming to bury your sister."

God, Aunt Celeste. I hadn't even gotten to talk to her in all this. Though, she had tried to call a time or two. I knew my dad had been talking to her as I heard her name a few times when he'd been tense on his cell phone last night. She was aware of what was going on, aware of my sister's death.

Dad glanced back at me. "So get your stuff together. I've already started the arrangements for your sister to be with your mom. They just need us, need us to bring her."

My mom and sister together. My mom and sister *buried* together at my mom's plot...

And so my own personal nightmare continued.

CHAPTER
THREE

Royal - Age 8

I whimpered, the sting making me rock. I needed to go inside.
I needed to get up.

Get up. Get up before someone finds out.

I couldn't, crying. It hurt so bad this time, and I gazed
down, the cut bleeding through my jacket sleeve. Through
burning tears, I peeled off my school jacket. The blood seeped
all the way through my white shirt and everything.

Oh, no.

I messed with the button until I rolled the sleeve up, biting
my lip so no one would hear my cries. I saw all the blood, and
I almost threw up. I couldn't even see the cut.

I started to touch it but stopped, feeling like I might
pass out.

What am I going to do?

"You're cut, kid."

A girl was out here with me, my height with dark braids
in her hair and even darker eyes. She smiled at me, on her

knees behind the tree with me. I didn't know how she'd found me. I'd been hiding, quiet.

I sniffed. "It's not bad." It wasn't bad. It could be worse.

Her smile fell as she pointed to my face. "You've been hit too."

I said nothing, my hand going to my hot cheek. I shook my head. "I fell."

She crawled toward me, on her knees in sneakers that weren't allowed. I'd tried to wear mine once to school and got yelled at. This girl must be new. I hadn't seen her before. She put out a hand. "Come on. Let's fix it."

How could she fix it? She wasn't a nurse or anything, and I'd have to go inside for that.

I stayed put, hesitant.

She crossed her arms, a red bandana tied around her neck like a cowboy. "Well, I guess if you want to stay out here by yourself all day, that's fine. I'm going to school."

She started to leave, and I got up too. I couldn't stay outside all day. I might get in trouble.

I held my arm and her smile came back. She took my wrist, guiding me out from behind the tree, and I let her take me to the school fountain. It looked like a dolphin in the midst of escape. It was leaving. It was swimming far away. There was a hose by the fountain the school's gardener used and she picked it up, unscrewing the sprayer off.

"Here," she said, putting my arm under running water from the hose. The initial sting made me jerk my arm back, but she merely smiled. She kept doing that at me, smiling. "It's okay. It'll feel better, okay?"

"Okay." I let her keep my arm under, closing my eyes so I wouldn't have to see all the blood. I didn't like blood. I hated it. I opened my eyes, and when I did, she didn't make me see the cut anymore. She'd placed the hose down, her bandana in her hands.

She tied it, right around my arm and the cut. She didn't care if I got blood on it for some reason. I'd care.

After she finished, she looked really proud of the job she did, and it was a good job. It didn't hurt anymore. Not even my face that had burned so bad.

"I'm Paige," she said, putting out a hand.

I took it, smiling too. "I'm Royal, Royal Prinze."

CHAPTER
FOUR

December - Present

Dad worked most of the trip from the Midwest to LA, falling back into old habits very quickly. He did the same thing after Mom died, on the phone or on the computer. His laptop had been completely secured to his lap in the first-class seats he provided for him and me, and I wished to God Rosanna had been able to come. She'd wanted to, grieving just as much as I was, but she had a family she went back to nightly. They needed her, regardless that Dad had offered to pay her way down with us. With her in Maywood Heights, she'd be caring for my dad's house as well as Hershey. A puppy along for this ride was just one more thing I'd have to juggle along with my emotions. Rosanna promised to FaceTime with me daily so I would at least see her and Hershey. Without Rosanna, that left my dad and me at the mercy of each other, something he completely avoided the entirety of our trip to bury my sister. Parental duties seemed optional as he more than took the hands-off approach to this trip. He had people to get our bags, drive us from the airport, get us food, and everything.

He did nothing for me or with me, the only words exchanged about service arrangements. My sister's remains would be cremated, then aired over to LA for a memorial service. He had it all taken care of.

All but the being-present part.

He abandoned me, at least mentally, and this was chillingly familiar. He'd taken a similar approach when Mom died, all that made easier when he and my sister moved halfway across the country.

I hugged my body in the back of a town car, traveling highways and streets I was more familiar with than where I actually lived. I stayed in LA because that's where our family had lived before our mom died from cancer...

My mom. It's just me and Dad now, isn't it?

My heart searing, I closed my eyes, hearing my dad beside me.

"You won't be wearing that to the service, will you?"

I turned to find him looking at me.

He tipped a chin in my direction. "Your nose piercing? It'll be inappropriate for such a formal event."

My sister wouldn't care how I looked.

Trying not to cry, I told him no, wondering now what was next for me. Now that my sister was gone I had no reason to stay with my dad. I could come back home, come... here. Paige would be here now, along with my mom.

I dampened my lips, silent all the way to Dad's Airbnb. He basically had us set up in a mini version of his own home, a housekeeper and everything, in the Hollywood Hills, and after getting our bags dropped off, my dad trekked to the LA slums with me, aka my aunt Celeste's place. She'd be waiting for us since she'd be coming along for our journey into the fucked-up process that was burying my only sister. She probably wouldn't have a say in the arrangements, all this my dad, but she was coming. She was adamant about that, and the reception would actually be at her house. Dad hadn't liked that one, and I heard him arguing with her most of last night about it on the phone. He must have lost that one because, as far as I knew, it was still happening.

People making this all about themselves…

Who knew if my dad or even my aunt cared about what my sister actually wanted. They hadn't cared about her, giving up on her. Maybe if they would have looked into her disappearance sooner like I had, she might be here right now, or at least found sooner.

I brought my legs up, cradling them as our sedan came to a stop. The driver opened my door and then my dad's, my father completely oblivious as he spouted off commands to someone.

"It better damn well be here by service time, or you can expect a lawsuit for the breech of contract," he said, then covered his phone. He nodded toward my aunt's place. "Go ahead and go on. These idiots in charge of your sister's arrangements got the wrong damn headstone."

I cringed, a chill behind his words. He'd been so cold about all this, everything regarding the process. This was obviously his way of coping, but I couldn't deal with things this way.

Getting out of the car, I slammed the door, rushing inside to see a face I desperately wanted to see. My aunt's car was in her driveway and mine too. She'd gone half on it with me for the old, beat-up Ford Focus. It barely ran, but it got the job done, and I'd hated to leave it. I'd hated to leave here, and I remembered that when I found my aunt in the living room. She'd been on the phone too, yelling at caterers from what it sounded like. I heard her say something about a fruit basket before spotting me at the door with my keys in hand.

My aunt was basically Mom's twin down to the wavy hair and being divinely beautiful, albeit always a bit stressed. She worked a lot, hard-working just like my mom. I'd pretty much raised myself when I'd lived here due to my aunt's busy schedule as a nurse, but that'd been okay. I was just happy she'd allowed me to stay at the time.

Her face flooded with relief when she saw me, and she lowered the phone, coming to me.

"Oh, honey," she said, gathering me up. We didn't hug a whole lot, but when we did, it always seemed to be over something tragic. I'd gotten an abortion my freshman year, and there'd been a lot of hugs then. My family just wasn't huggers, that'd been my sister's job.

I ached I wouldn't get those anymore, my aunt's hand coming down my hair before pulling away.

"How are you doing?" she asked, then shook her head. "Stupid question. Sorry."

It wasn't a stupid question. It was an instinctual one. I swallowed. "All right, I guess."

She took that for what it was, framing my face. She looked around. "Where's your dad?"

"In the car. Yelling at someone. It sounds like he's mad at the funeral hall."

This made her face screw up, her expression souring. I didn't want to say she hated my dad since that was such a strong word, but when Mom died and he so easily gave me up to live with her, she hadn't been happy. She wanted him to step up back then, be a dad to me and Paige. He hadn't really been one to my sister either, regardless of the fact that Paige lived in his house, and Aunt Celeste knew that too. She nodded. "Typical of him. Where are your bags?"

After explaining how Dad had us staying at an Airbnb and *not* with my mom's only sister, I got another "typical" directed my dad's way and found myself happy he stayed outside for the moment. I had a feeling there'd be a lot of this back-and-forth.

"Well, we're going to talk about that," she finished with, then rubbed my shoulders. "And what's going to happen after all this? I can imagine you're staying here? With me? Your room's just how you left it."

Since I hadn't decided that yet, I couldn't tell her, and it seemed she didn't need an answer right away because my dad decided to grace us with his presence. Phone in hand, he'd at least wrapped up his call, but that was only before getting another upon passing the threshold of my aunt's place.

"Celeste," he murmured, covering up his line.

She grimaced. "Rowan. I see you're involved in every-thing but actually helping your grieving daughter inside. You plan on being present while you're here or…?"

He grunted, mumbling something about not needing all this "during this time," and when my aunt left my side to step up to him, I figured that was my signal to get the fuck out. I went down the hall, avoiding all the bullshit, but even after I slammed the door to my room, I only heard more.

"Well, now you've done it," I heard from my aunt, my ear pressed to the door. "Father of the year."

"And you're definitely helping, Celeste."

"Rowan—"

I cut off the noise when I opened my window, then climbed out. On my belly, my phone buzzed from inside my pocket. Touching ground, I pulled my phone out, and I sagged against the house, relieved when I saw who texted.

Royal: You make it to LA okay?

I closed my eyes, more tears for some reason. I think I was just emotional with all this, all the tension just too much on top of it all. He had a way of somehow making perfect timing, and I lowered to the ground, sitting in the grass.

Me: Yeah, just got in. My aunt and dad are going at it.

Royal: I'm sorry it's like that. I'm sorry for all this.

Maybe *sorry*s were things people just said when things were shitty, something of an obligation. For whatever reason, he couldn't stop.

Me: Stop apologizing. This isn't your fault.

Royal: We were out there together. It is my fault.

Me: She was drunk, and we both know Paige Lindquist can't be controlled.

Royal: I could have controlled her. I could have if I tried harder.

Me: I don't think so. This isn't your fault, so just stop.

He didn't say anything for a moment, and I almost texted him again until I saw the text message bubble hit.

Royal: I'm coming down soon, but I won't be able to make the memorial service. Probably just the reception.

My heart sank. He'd been invited, something I made sure my dad did along with his plans.

Me: Why?

Royal: I want to be there, but I have to handle something. It came up suddenly, and the timing just won't work out.

But Paige was his best friend, all this really important.

My finger hovering, I wondered if all this was an excuse, that he couldn't deal with this and just didn't want to say. When my mom died, I hadn't even been able to look into the casket, all of it too painful even at the age I'd been.

Royal: Em?

Me: I'm here. Just disappointed. Paige would have wanted you here.

Royal: I will be. Just not for the service and the burial. The guys will be there, though, and I won't miss the reception. I fucking promise.

Why did it feel so good to know they'd all be coming down? Royal, Jax, LJ, and even the near silent Knight had somehow become my family when they'd been my sister's. They'd be a buffer with all this bullshit. They'd be *my* family.

I started to type something, saying I missed him, but then backtracked. I didn't want to sound as desperate as I felt.

Me: Good. I'm glad.

Royal: You'll be okay. I'll make sure of it, Em.

He felt he had so much power in things he had no control over, his position at school and in Maywood Heights making him think so. I'd seen firsthand how the beautiful boy with green eyes even made adults submit in his wake, my dad included. I texted Royal a few more things about the location of the service arrangements and where I was staying. I knew he was aware of most of that since he got an invitation, but just in case he could get here sooner, I wanted him to have the details. After we were done, a flood of text messages coming in let me know my texts were finally catching up with me now that I was on the ground. I had my phone on airplane mode when I'd been in the air.

Birdie: How are you doing, friend?

I'd gotten similar contact from other connections I'd made in Maywood Heights. I didn't make a whole lot of them, but Birdie and the Windsor Prep female basketball team had been a few. Kiki and Shakira, Birdie's other friends and teammates on the team, reached out to me too. They were all supposed to be coming down for my sister's service, the beauty of going to a school full of rich kids. I had no idea who'd all be showing up to this thing, but considering Maywood Heights seemed to be all about making statements with one's money and influence, I was sure the guest list would be extensive.

Me: I've been better. Miss you guys.

Birdie: We miss you too. Hang in there, and we're here for you. Just know that when you make it back home, you have friends.

Home. I didn't know where that was for me at the present, and I stood, facing the window. I was on the ground, and my aunt and dad were still going at it inside.

Who knew if they even knew I was gone?

CHAPTER
FIVE

December

So the next few days were the worst. If not *the* worst of my entire goddamn life. They were full of traditions and bullshit adults made us do for appearances and other crap. I had to be present. I had to watch as my sister's remains arrived in a box and were passed around like it was just an urn and not a person in there. I had to submit and sit there for decisions that were made around me, things that didn't matter like what flowers looked good where and if the music would be right for that particular point in the service. I had to sit and stay silent. I had to keep my mouth shut, and not once had I been asked about what I thought about any of it. No one asked what Paige would think about any of it either, the service a perfect replica of our late mother's. I mean, down to the damn decorations on the pews. They kept a picture of my sister in the front of the church, her urn right in front of it. She'd been wearing her lacrosse uniform, the urn shiny and polished before they placed it in the ground. I hadn't gotten close to it, unable to do so. Instead, I took my seat at the back of the church the day of. I stayed there while everything happened around me all morning. At one point, my aunt discovered me, but I told her I wasn't moving. I couldn't get any closer.

I couldn't see my sister that way.

Closing off, I held my body as that church filled up, people from both my past and present filtering in. Some of my old friends had showed, ones from my old life and this place. Of course they found me, gave me hugs, and condolences, but I hadn't given them much back. When I didn't, they went about their way, blending into the crowd, and soon, I didn't even have to be a part of the condolences. The crowds hid me. I blended into the scenery of the floral arrangements and beautiful music, a statement piece like the rest of it all.

I wished this goddamn thing was over.

It didn't seem to end, so many people around me and not one of them I wanted to see. The one person I did want to see wasn't here, and ultimately, Jax, Knight, and LJ arrived by themselves when they came into the wide church. Royal wasn't with them at all, unable to make it like he said. I figured once the guys found me they'd come over, and they did spot me, Jax first. I rose up, happy to see at least them, but then something weird happened. Almost automatically, Jax started to come over.

But LJ held him back.

He physically put a hand on his chest, speaking to him lightly. After that, Jax simply nodded at me, the other two as well, before going to the front of the church. I didn't know what that was about, sitting down, but figured maybe they knew I was hiding in the back for a reason.

Yeah, that has to be it.

It was the only thing that made sense, and I watched the

boys, the guys heading up to the front. They stood as a line, just staring at my sister's picture. They wouldn't look at her urn at all, a lot like me, and eventually, Jax wasn't having any more of it. He turned away, and when he did, the other guys went with him. *That* almost got me, watching LJ put a hand to the jokester's shoulder and rub when they took their seats. LJ himself held up his head, and turning, Knight spoke to Jax. Almost right away, Jax shook it off, sitting tall too. Boys, they probably didn't want to show a lot of emotion, even for their good friend.

I swallowed, trying to be happy about the fact they left me to my peace. That's what I wanted after all, seclusion, so I stayed put while I got it. I continued to people watch, and soon, more of my people came into the room, Birdie, Shakira, and Kiki. All tall, they elevated above the crowd, and Kiki, her dark hair flowing down her back like a cloak, gestured the group my way. She looked lovely, they all did in their black cocktail dresses, and I wore something similar. The only difference was I wore my hair down, deliberate and wavy to hide my face. Shakira had the most unique style, her hair in thick braids, while Birdie wore a bun within her dark hair. Birdie led the party over, and when she did, the hugs were nonstop. They each took a turn, and after, Birdie sat next to me.

"Hey," she said.

"Hi," I returned, my mouth dry. I think they were the first words I'd said in quite a bit of time. I had no desire, no strength, and I think the girls quickly figured that out.

"I think we'll just sit," Birdie said, looking at the others. "Just sit."

The words were obviously said for me, and after telling them that was okay, we did. We just sat. We watched as the church became a cluster-fuck of pomp and circumstance. Half my school came out from Windsor Prep, teachers included,

and so many people I'd never even met. I was sure Paige
didn't have any connections with them either.

This is all my dad.

He had his hands in everything, taking his seat at the front
of the church eventually. He looked around after he did,
seemingly searching for something, and my aunt next to him,
leaned over. She whispered something that had him suddenly
turning his head, and when he made direct eye contact with
me, frowning like I did something wrong here on this day, I
gazed away. He couldn't guilt me into anything I didn't want
to do. Not today. I was sitting back here, no negotiations.

I stared ahead, wishing this thing would be over. We still
had the internment of ashes and reception after this. God...

"Who's that woman?" I found myself asking Birdie, a
woman at my sister's urn. Why she took my attention when
the others hadn't was because of what she did when she went
up front.

She put her hand on my sister's urn, cradling it with a
tissue to her face. She stayed for a long time, holding up the
line.

"The headmaster's wife," Birdie said, all of us watching as
the headmaster himself showed for this too. Principal Hastings came up behind her, whispering something to her before
guiding her away. She didn't go quickly, the woman as shiny
and beautiful as everyone and everything else in Maywood
Heights. She had her black hair down, chunky curls making
her look like a goddess. She didn't wear black like everyone
else, but navy, the lovely silk trailing behind her when Principal Hastings finally got her away and to sit behind my dad.
Dad had quite a party there, no room for me even if I wanted
to be there. Besides close family, he had what I assumed were
Maywood Heights people. They dressed the nicest, the most
polished.

Birdie looked at me. "She used to be the school's guidance
counselor my freshman year."

I was sure she'd seen my sister quite a lot, then, even back then. Paige and my dad had been going at it since long before I could remember, just their relationship.

I sat back, Birdie pointing out more people to me including the mayor of Maywood Heights and his wife. They all sat with my dad, grieving with him when they gave him a touch on the shoulder or a hand. Dad had obviously created some connections there I hadn't known about.

Me: Are you close? Please tell me you are.

My text from Royal went unreturned, and if he were traveling, he wouldn't be able to text anyway unless he was in town. He left me to deal with this by myself.

At least, that's what it felt like.

———

The internment of the ashes was just for family and close friends, and unfortunately, I had to be a part of that, standing between my aunt and dad as his people placed my sister in her final resting place. I had to watch then, made myself. I stood near my mother's remains while my sister was lowered in the ground beside her. I stood by idle, not allowing her voice to be heard as the minister talked about a girl who'd had a bright future and said words my dad no doubt wrote for the sake of tradition and all these people. It disgusted me a little bit, the lack of thought and care. I guess that just remained consistent when it came to her life. No one had been there for her, not even me in the end.

I lit a joint outside my aunt's house, not particularly caring about the implications of it. My dad hadn't given a fuck about me this whole trip anyway, my aunt even less. When I was around them both, they were fighting, couldn't even keep it together for a goddamn minute, about things that didn't matter. They didn't ask if I was okay or if I needed anything. They just fought and quibbled about bullshit.

I finished my smoke and then went inside, deciding to do another circulation of the house. A lot of people had come and gone, eating my aunt's food saying things like what a tragedy all this was. People gave me their fake smiles when they never once talked to me in school or in life, my new world and my old world colliding around me. People showed from both worlds I didn't want to talk to and were no doubt here just for the gossip.

The gossip…

I watched that flitter through as well, people talking. They usually stopped when I came through and I figured it was either about my sister or me.

I hoped the latter.

I lingered by the pie table, spotting Jax, LJ, and Knight across the room, but again no Royal. They eventually said something to me, but it'd been brief at my sister's burial. They'd been invited to that because I asked my dad. I got a hand on the shoulder from each of them, and again, Jax wanted to do more, but the other guys had pulled him away. Like, they physically tugged at his jacket. They kept him back like I had a disease, and once more, I got wanting to give me my space but it was too weird, and that distance continued at my aunt's house. They talked to other people, other Court guys and such, but not to me. I didn't get it, and there was *still* no Royal either. I mean, he was supposed to be her best friend, wasn't he? And I hoped, even though I didn't know what we were to each other, he'd kind of be here for me too.

Me: Where the hell are you?

He hadn't answered my text at the church, and when I looked up, I found three sets of eyes on me. Any Court boys would stand out in the crowd, so Jax, LJ, and Knight were no exception. They were just as big, powerful, and beautiful as Royal Prinze, and they knew it just like Royal Prinze. They watched me from time to time during my circulations, like they were keeping tabs on me, but I doubted it. They stopped talking like everyone else when I'd been around.

So much for family.

They said as much to me at homecoming, but maybe something had changed. Maybe my sister's death meant I could no longer be a part of their club, their mascot cut off and tossed out. I didn't give a fuck anyway. I didn't give a fuck about any of this. I started to go back outside but stopped when I caught a glance through the living room window. There were lots of people out there, but I recognized the two easily, fiery red hair and a beautiful boy. Royal Prinze was outside my aunt's house.

And he was with Mira.

The girl literally had it out for me in the past, a complete bitch, and I only saw red. She hadn't been at the memorial.

Had they come together?

I had to question that as they spoke to each other now, Royal in a black suit and dark tie. He had his hands in his pockets, his expression tense as Mira spoke to him. They spoke for quite a long time before Mira dismissed herself, putting a hand on Royal's arm before leaving him. I figured she'd make a beeline right inside and I really didn't want to see her, get her fake-ass condolences.

Swallowing, I headed to my old bedroom, closing myself in. I placed my head back to the wall.

"I suppose you're wanting her back here, then? Back with you?"

I opened my eyes at the sound of my dad's voice, my aunt's room on the other side.

"I told her she could, told her as much. She knows she's welcome back here."

I cradled my legs, my aunt and dad obviously wanted to talk away from everyone else, away from me.

"But I think you need to step up this time, Rowan," she continued. "A relationship with you is what's best for her, and yes, I have the space, but I work. I work a lot, and it's hard. I love her, but I have put my life on hold, always have when your daughter should be with you."

I closed my eyes, a burn in my throat and eyes I hadn't expected. I'd heard conversations like this before. She never meant for me to hear them, but I had. It was no secret my aunt loved me like she said, but she had made sacrifices.

A heavy breath came from the other side of the wall.

"I can't give her what she needs," my dad said, the ache ripping raw through my chest. "I don't... She should be here. I don't have time to deal with it, her and everything she needs right now."

"Hey."

Royal shut the door behind himself, coming into my room and how much he took up of it. His blond hair was tousled but purposeful this time, perfectly fallen and placed with no doubt restless fingers. The buttons of his dress shirt labored as he slid hands into his pockets. "Why are you hiding in here?"

I was hiding, hiding from everyone but him.

It all was a blur when I got up, launching myself from the bed and into his arms, and how quickly he opened up for me. He braced me, cradling the back of my head.

"Em..." he said, breathing me in, and how my body shivered at just the way he said my name. He brought me home and took me to a place where it was just him and me.

I secured my arms around his neck, crying way too much around this boy. I couldn't help it. This whole day... my whole life was bullshit. He seemed to be the only thing that wasn't, here and now and cared.

"Let's get out of here," I said, pleading. "Let's just fucking go. Go somewhere, anywhere."

I didn't know what I was saying to him or even what I meant. I just wanted him to take me away.

He pulled back a little, thumb stroking my cheek. "Go where?"

"I don't know. I just need to go. We can get bus tickets. Just go."

"Bus tickets?" His eyes questioned me, his voice. "You want to leave, leave?"

Why not? He had with Paige. He said they just left in the past, took off and said to hell with everything.

"You did with Paige," I said, my hands moving down to his lapels. "I need to get out. My dad doesn't want me. I make my aunt's life bullshit. She doesn't want me. I don't belong anywhere."

The tears flew down, hot and warm as his hands on my body. He shook his head. "Em…"

"Why can't we just leave, huh? We should go. Paige is gone. We should just go."

"Where?"

"I don't know. Like I said, anywhere." I knew this sounded completely and utterly crazy. I didn't know him well, and he didn't know me, but didn't we? We had that connection through my sister. We knew each other *through* my sister. We could figure the rest of everything else out later.

He watched me, a tension around his eyes I hadn't noticed until I finally looked really at him. It, all over his face, consumed him, but he cut me off from it when he stared out my window. There were people there, three in particular.

Jax, LJ, and Knight drank something from cups, not alone as there were others outside with them. They were with a group of boys, all of them wearing Court rings. I'd seen a few of them multiple times throughout the day. All the guys were in conversation, but Knight, LJ, and Jax were curiously absent. The three didn't make a big deal about it during the conversation, but I noticed their eyes sliding over to the direction of Royal and me. They watched us, knew we were in here at least.

A hand fell into mine, and I was pulled away from it all. Royal kissed my hand.

"I'll take care of it," he said, then tugged me close. His mouth fell hot, heavy on my lips, and I felt every breath, every taste. He guided my mouth open, his eyes closed when he moved to my ear. "We'll leave in the morning."

CHAPTER
SIX

December

Royal's text came around midnight. He wanted me to meet him at the local bus station in the morning. We were going to leave.

The time would be eight o'clock.

I wished I considered backtracking the decision more but I didn't. I both wanted and needed to get out of everywhere having to do with Maywood Heights, my dad, and even my aunt. My sister and what happened to her haunted me and threatened to completely crush my sanity. I wanted escape. I wanted relief, and Royal was providing that. He had us going out to somewhere in Arizona according to his text message. I didn't know if he knew people there or what, but whatever the case, he was getting me out of here. That's all I needed. I packed a bag, left a note for my dad in the morning, and then I was off. I told him I just needed some space and did thank him for letting me stay with him for the time he did. I felt I owed him that, but that was about it. My aunt I'd give a little more to once Royal and I got far out of town. I planned to call her, give her something. Though, I didn't know what. She'd taken care of me, but now I was relieving her of her burden. She could live her life, both she and my dad could. As far as my baby girl, my little Labrador in another town, I planned to ask the biggest favor from a good friend. Rosanna was already taking care of her, and I had a strong feeling she'd continue to do so. For how long, I didn't know. I honestly wanted Hershey with me, but at the present, that wasn't possible. I hoped Rosanna could help me out and I'd be calling her too once I got settled.

Birdie: I'm so sorry we didn't get to talk more yesterday. I figured you wanted your space.

I'd seen Birdie, Shakira, and Kiki at my sister's reception, but hadn't really talked to any of them. I hadn't talked to hardly anyone, hiding most of the day. I felt I owed my friends too from Maywood Heights, but currently, wasn't in a state to explain anything I was doing today to anyone.

I gazed up, currently sitting on a bench outside the bus station. I waited for Royal Prinze, a running bus before me but he hadn't arrived yet.

Me: You're completely fine and a great friend. Thank you for that yesterday and to Kiki and Shakira too. Thank them for me?

Birdie: Sure will, and you're welcome. You're just so strong. Stronger than me, girl, to be going through this.

I didn't know how strong I was, running away, but this was the only way I could deal with all this *stuff*, all of it too much.

Birdie: Hey, um, you free right now? I know it's early and I know you've got plenty of things going on, but the girls and I would love to do breakfast. We're all leaving this morning but want to see you first.

A running bus in front of me, breakfast definitely wasn't an option, and if I weren't leaving in moments, I didn't know if I had the strength to look at them in their faces prior to departure. Escape was easier if one didn't have to stare the people she cared about in the eyes.

I studied my phone time, rocking back and forth.

Where are you, Royal?

Me: I can't, and yeah, unfortunately busy.

Before I had time to process what I sent, my phone rang in my hands, Birdie. Picking up was not an option, but when she called again, I broke down. "Hello?"

"Hey, hi."

"Hi, what's going on?"

Birdie paused before speaking this time, a nice long pause, and I had to check the phone to make sure she was still there.

"I really hate doing this on the phone," she started, anxiety bursting within me for some reason. I think with all the stress I was already on edge, but her lead-in didn't help. A swallow hit the phone. "But if I can't see you today, I don't want you to come back to town not knowing. If people are talking about something, I want you to know."

"What?" I sat up, my heart racing now.

"There was talk yesterday, December."

"What kind of talk?" I asked, adjusting my bag on my lap.

"Things were said, conversations going on in the midst of everything. Anyway, people were talking, talking about you and... some stuff that happened before you went to our school."

Reality spun around me, the world quite literally turning on its axis. "What did you hear?"

Silence for a moment, but then a sigh. "I really hate doing this over the phone."

Then make yourself. Please...

I waited, my breath bated, and I had to hear. I had to hear her *say* whatever it was she believed she knew.

"People were saying you had an abortion."

The words were light, but I heard them, my bag falling off my lap as I folded fingers over my eyes. "Who told you?"

A soft gasp hit the phone, reality hitting for her as well. Maybe, before this call she held out that what she heard had been a rumor, not as true as I sat on this bench ready to leave the rest of the world fucking behind.

"I, we, the girls and I, heard from some Court-kept girls," she hurried. "Who I think heard from some people at your old school."

I buried my face in my arms, falling deeper into the depths than I already was. I knew people from my new school finding out about my abortion was a possibility, but with everything else going on yesterday...

"Does everyone know?" I retched, looking up, looking for Royal. Where the fuck was he?

"I think so. I'm so sorry, December."

"You almost ready, little lady? Bus leaves in ten."

The bus driver was midway down the stairs, her face in a frown as she stared at me. It was apparently time to go, and here I was without a bus ticket, without *Royal* and I didn't understand.

But maybe now I did.

"I have to go, Birdie. I'm so sorry."

"Wait, December. Can we talk—"

I cut her off, hanging up. I had to call Royal. If he heard about this, if he heard and that's why he wasn't here...

"Miss?" the bus driver asked.

"Just two seconds. I need just two seconds, please." I stood, my phone to my ear. "I don't have my ticket and the person who's bringing it is coming too."

Her frown deepened. "You've only got two seconds. Seriously, we're leaving on time."

I nodded, grabbing my bag as I walked into the street. The phone started to ring, but I shut if off the moment a black sedan pulled up to the curb in front of me. I recognized the person inside.

It just wasn't Royal.

LJ got out of what appeared to be a rented car, the Hertz sticker in the window. He was very much *by himself*, his sunglasses on, which he took off the moment he saw me. He walked toward me, meeting me halfway, and I put my phone away.

"What's going on?" I asked, gazing around him. No one had been in that car but him. "Why are you here? Where's Royal? Did he tell you we were leaving?"

LJ dampened his lips, pushing sunglasses into the fluffy, blond hair that currently rested on his shoulders. He had nothing on Royal's spun gold even with the length, not many could. LJ pocketed his hands. "He, uh, he sent me, Lindquist."

My insides fluttered, my jaw tight and tense. "Why?"

He couldn't look at me after I asked that question, his eyes completely averted.

"Why, LJ?"

He scratched into his hair, then tucked his hands under his arms. "Because he's not coming."

I couldn't breath, couldn't... see. "What are you talking about?"

Maybe he thought visuals were better than words because out of his pocket suddenly came a ticket, just one. The ticket fluttering in the wind, I noticed a single name and it wasn't Royal's.

I stared at the ticket, *my name* on it and apparently headed for a town in Arizona I'd never heard of. I shook my head. "Why is he doing this?"

His lips closed to that, jaw working before he waved the ticket at me. He urged it. "He said he's sorry. He's sorry, but he thinks you should go."

He thinks I should go...

"Why?" I challenged, and when he said nothing again, I stood up to him. "Did he hear something? Does he know something?"

"December—"

"Is it the abortion?" I asked flat out. "Is that it? Is that what he heard because… Christ, LJ. I'd never try to trap him or something."

"It's not that."

I blanched. "What is it, then?"

All of this was completely awkward for him, clearly when he pushed his hand over his hair. "It's all just too much, you know?" he stated, that hurting more than something else for some reason. I didn't know why but it did. He breathed hard. "Things with you and him… they just got too hot, and he didn't want to hurt your feelings—"

"You're lying. You're lying!"

"I'm not, December," he rushed, completely serious. "And God do I wish I was. You think I like hurting you? You're Paige's sister. You're family."

Some fucking family. All of them completely ignored me yesterday, avoided me like the plague and I was diseased. They didn't care about me.

And apparently, neither did Royal.

Taking LJ's ticket, I walked away.

"December…"

"Fuck you." I shot around, tears in my eyes. I wiped them away. "Fuck *all* of you, and pass that on to Royal too."

His lips closed, and though he had no reason, he didn't follow me. He let me walk away and get on that bus that was about to leave. He let me *leave* and said to hell with anything regarding family. I guess that's how things were going to be, the decision about what was next for me I guess made.

CHAPTER
SEVEN

Royal - Age 9

"Oh my *Goddd*, you're going to be doing that forever. Let me."

Hands came around me, helping me with my tie. Paige had been playing video games, a new thing I got in the mail from Grandma and Grandpa. They sent things all the time, knowing my dad. Knowing he didn't remember things like birthdays and stuff.

Paige didn't wrestle with my tie like I had for the last hour or something. She got it right like a wizard, the thing perfect when she stepped back.

"How did you know how to do that?" I asked, shocked when I straightened it.

She shrugged in her bib overalls. "I watched my dad. He wears one every day."

I adjusted it again. It had to be perfect. Dad would be mad if it wasn't.

"I don't want to go to this," I confessed, but she knew. I always had to go to parties, but this was the first Court party. All the dads and uncles and everything came. I'd been hearing about the Court and what it was my whole life, and now that I was nine, they were making me go. I frowned. "Can't you come with?"

It was a stupid thing to ask her, and if she were a boy, she'd already be getting ready for it. Why couldn't she have been a boy?

She threw an arm around me, staring at the pair of us in the mirror. If it wasn't for her ponytail, she could get by as just one of my friends. She was one of my friends, right there with LJ, Jax, Knight, and me. We were together all the time, and Paige wasn't a girl when she was with us. She was just one of our friends.

"I'd love to go, Royal Prinze," she said, surprising me. Her dark eyes danced. "I would if I had something to wear. But since I don't…"

"You could," I said, looking at her. "Are you serious? Because if you are, I have something." I had many things, and I took her hand, running out of the game room and through the house. Our butler Graves gave me an eye, but didn't stop me. I ran through the house all the time. Especially when I knew Dad wasn't home. He was already at Windsor House for my presentation to the other members tonight. I'd been hearing about it for months.

It all has to be perfect.

And it would be with all my friends there, Paige. The guys would be there, LJ, Jax, and Knight, but she needed to be there too. It wasn't fair if she couldn't go just because she was a girl and no one ever said girls couldn't go. They just never tried.

I brought her into a room uncovered with dust, but the stillness, the silence still felt like there were ghosts. I didn't go in here, wasn't allowed in here, but we only needed to borrow something.

I turned on the light, making Paige's eyes adjust as well as mine. The chandelier glistened over the pink quilt on the bed, cherubs and angels decorating the ceiling like out of a story-book. My mom designed it. She'd loved it in here.

I went to the closest, opening it up. So many dresses were in there, perfect still as our housekeepers make sure they were. I plucked a red one, perfect for Paige.

"Wow," she said, accepting it. She held it up to herself. "How does it look?"

So not like my friend, but not in a bad way. I laughed since she didn't wear dresses.

She did too, grinning. We both went over to the mirror, and she danced with it, spinning around while she held the dress up to herself.

"Will you go tonight?" I asked, daring. "Now that you have something to wear?" I hoped she was serious. I didn't like when people lied. People lied to me a lot and thought they could because they are older. I always knew though. I could always see it in their eyes.

Paige chewed her lip a little, the playfulness leaving from her eyes. "Where did this come from, Royal? I mean, who do all these belong to? The dresses?"

My heart squeezed, and I looked at us both in the mirror.

"They were my sister's," I confessed.

Her eyes widened, her swallow hard. "You had a sister?"

I nodded, watching as she lowered the dress. I got scared she might not go now, that all this would be weird for her. She didn't know I had a sister. She just knew about my mom.

I guess I had to tell her about all that now.

I thought she'd ask me right away about my sister but she didn't. Instead, she grabbed my hand, pushing me out of the room.

"I have to get dressed, silly," she said, grinning. "You're taking me to a ball."

CHAPTER
EIGHT

December - Present

"Hey, bitch! Come back here!"

I ran, the loot in my pocket as I put distance between myself and the convenience store. Thank God I stashed my bag in an alley. I never would have been able to run with it.

"Get your ass back here and pay for that!"

I didn't, the warm-colored streets of Arizona a blur as I searched for someplace to take refuge. I couldn't go back for my bag, not yet with this guy chasing me. I hadn't seen him when I decided to pocket some grain bars and a few snacks. I hadn't thought at all really. I'd just been hungry, and that hunger caused me to do something stupid. Rounding a corner and nearly clipping a pedestrian, I came across a street naked of people. If that shop owner followed me here, he'd see wherever I went.

I scanned the area like an agent, making a quick decision to shove myself into the nearest store, and as soon as I did, I pressed the door shut behind me. The chime went off, a damn chime that could give me away. I fled from the door like it'd marked me.

"We're closed," shot a voice from somewhere inside the place, and I attempted to be casual, a hand on the stolen shit in my pocket as I approached a shelf of books. Some kind of bookstore. I shuffled around.

"I said we're..." The boy came out of the shelves, a tall boy with honey-tanned skin and a beanie that covered a wash of dark curls. He had a stack of books in his hands, a curious look in his eyes as he approached in tight, black jeans and a slouchy tee. He slid the books on a shelf. "We're closing soon. Can I help you with something...?"

He'd stopped because of the voice, the shouting outside his store taking both our attention.

"I'm gonna find you, bitch!" came from outside, the man who'd been chasing me right outside the door. I saw him well through the bookstore's glass. He turned, hands on his head. "You don't steal from my fucking store and get away with it!"

He stood there for a second, my heart in my throat as I hoped to God he didn't take his search just a smidgen to his left. He need only look through the glass to find what he sought for, but as it turned out, someone gave me a break today. Shaking his head, the shop owner continued on down the street, and I closed my eyes.

"So um, if you've come to steal something, you don't have to. This is a library, so just check out whatever you want."

Shit.

I gazed up at the boy that currently eyed me like a criminal. I guess he wasn't far off. I had stolen something, but I felt I had no choice. I was down to my last few dollars, and hell if I'd stoop to using my dad's credit cards. I still had them, but I had a feeling a squad car wouldn't be far behind. He couldn't really do anything, since I was eighteen when I left, but if he knew where I was, he might come for me.

I pulled my hoodie sleeves up my arms. "I wasn't going to

steal anything. Just wanted to see if I could use the computer." Since this was a library, he should have one, a good excuse.

The boy pursed his lips, clearly in debate here. In the end, I figured he decided to give me what I wanted. He pocketed hands. "You've got fifteen minutes. It's in the back. Password for the lock screen is 'Call me Ishmael.'"

A *Moby Dick* quote, cute, but I didn't linger. I headed toward the back through the books, the tiniest library I'd ever seen in possibly the tiniest town I'd ever been in. Maywood Heights wasn't huge, but it was bigger than this. I wondered quite a few times over the past two weeks I'd been here why Royal had decided to give me a bus ticket to this town out of anywhere.

He wanted you buried. He wanted to bury you.

He wanted me away. He didn't want *me* and no doubt had freaked out about the whole abortion news. It was the only thing that made sense, which was stupid. That had nothing to do with him. Whenever I thought about all that, him, and how he'd handled things by letting LJ come to me, thoughts of *fuck them all* came to mind. After that, I let myself stop caring. I had to in order to move on with my life and the day. I stopped caring about a lot of things since getting on that bus, but one of the few I still did was the subject of an email I got when I used the library boy's password to get onto the computer. I got to see how my baby was doing today, finally.

Rosanna had attached a picture of Hershey to her email this evening, Hershey and her. We used to FaceTime. That was until my phone died. I had no charger, and since I couldn't currently afford one, all contact these days was through the local internet cafe. I usually logged on there to check into the rest of the world. They had a couple computers.

"We're both doing well," Rosanna's email said, my saving grace and how she'd tried to talk me off that bus when I

called. It'd been the first thing I did when I got on, wanting Hershey to be okay. She took her in, of course, but only after asking me a million questions I still refused to answer. No, I couldn't tell her where I was. No, I wouldn't be coming home, and no, I didn't care about how my dad felt about it. He tried to tell me several times with phone calls I didn't pick up, texts and the like. Aunt Celeste did the same thing, but the two weren't getting anything from me. They said how they felt, and I'd heard it in bounds the day of my sister's memorial service. They both could move on to living their lives now that they didn't have me anymore, and wasn't that what they wanted? Others had been a little harder, Shakira, Kiki, and especially Birdie. I didn't call Birdie right after I ended our call, and she freaked out. She kept calling, kept texting, and the others too. Eventually, I answered them all. I explained I was staying in LA, was busy, which was why I didn't get back to them right away. I felt I had to lie to them so they would back of, but they didn't. They came with more questions.

My phone couldn't have died any sooner.

"They wrote up a nice piece about your sister today in the paper. I attached it. Please check in soon, and I can send you money for a phone charger if that's what you need. I can even send you a charger if you send me your address," Rosanna's email continued. I flat-out refused to take any money from her, and she'd unfortunately have no place to send the latter, considering I was homeless. I was getting by staying at the local shelter, but with my altercation at the local convenience store, I cruised right past the hour to get in there tonight. I was on my own this evening.

Wouldn't be the first time, I guess.

My attention drifted to the news article Rosanna referenced, my heart squeezing. I opened it but couldn't quite read it, not ready.

"One minute."

My verbal alarm came behind me, the boy as he stepped from behind the bookshelves. He had on one of those bags guys strapped across their chests, a set of keys in his hand. "I'm locking up."

He looked a little young to be running a library, but could have been older than me. I couldn't really gauge his ethnicity on looks alone, but most people were a lot darker than me out here in the desert. If I had to guess, I would have said white mixed with something else. Maybe even a few something elses. The Hispanic population was more prevalent in this area, so that was a possibility.

My time up, I asked if I could print something before I left and he charged me ten cents a page. I guess this was one of those emergencies.

CHAPTER
NINE

December

I had a long night ahead of me, a long night of wandering the streets and trying to keep warm. It got surprisingly cool out in the desert, and I eventually took my travels beneath a bridge, a few others there too, bundled up. They had a turned-over trash can or two with fire in the center, but I stayed away from those, letting others keep warm. I'd never camped out here before, but why I chose the place at all was because I saw kids. They were curled up with a woman, and I stayed near them, safety in numbers.

The woman watched me, smiling a little, but she did hold her kids close. I didn't blame her. They didn't know who I was at all, and for all I knew, she could shank me in the middle of the night. I kept my distance, using my shoulder bag to sit on as I curled myself up into my hoodie. I unsheathed one of my stolen grain bars, still managing to stay vegan out here. It was actually harder to be omni if one could imagine. Anything animal product related required heat to eat, and since I didn't want that anyway, I was good. I got by on whole foods for the most part, the initial stash I bought with the cash I first arrived with holding me over for quite a few days before I started panicking. I'd recently started to ration. Hence, the stealing.

I wet my lips, trying not to fall into the depths of my decisions. If I did, I thought about all of them, my sister and Royal included. It was best to stay present, but I couldn't help going down memory lane when I unfolded the printed paper from the article Rosanna sent me. I wanted to see my sister.

And I sure did see her.

She was so lively, her face already starting to fade from my memories. The paper was a memorial piece, the life and times of a youth gone too soon. That town didn't care about her, probably just wanting a story. In the lead-up to the memorial, all kinds of things came out in the papers, major publications too considering how it happened. They'd been slandering my sister, saying how reckless and broken she was, the result being what happened to her. I didn't read them all, but I read enough, washing my hands of it all before this.

I brushed my hand over her image, my sister smiling in her Windsor Prep uniform with her books in hand like she actually liked school and classes. The paper had quotes from other people, "friends," they said but not one of them was Royal and the guys.

Until they were.

They had so many pictures of them together on page three, all of them, Jax, LJ, Knight, Royal...

My throat thickened at seeing Royal's arm around her, *happy with her* and not so stone-faced. She was happy too, the two in their sports uniforms and running across fields together. In fact, there were so many photos I thought maybe Royal may have submitted some of them.

That would require him to be a decent person.

"*Things with you and him... they just got too hot.*"

I called bullshit on that. I called bullshit on it all. I hadn't known what Royal and I were, but not once had I ever pressured him. Yeah, I asked him to go away together, but he didn't have to. He had a choice.

I guess he made it in the end.

I hadn't cried since that day, not once. I hadn't wanted to give him the satisfaction. Tears showed I actually cared. Tears showed he mattered to me.

Sniffling, I moved on from his photos with my sister, trying to read what they were saying about Paige herself. My eyes blurred with tears, I finally came across some photos without Royal and the rest. My sister was young, really young. Maybe freshman year? Paige was in the hallway with a few girls and a woman I'd seen before. Birdie had said she was the headmaster's wife.

The woman wore a necklace, a silver emblem. Her arm around Paige and the rest of the girls—the caption read, *Mrs. Hastings (former guidance counselor at Windsor Preparatory) and other students from Windsor Preparatory remember a valued student.*

The article had quotes from those other students, all of them saying nice things.

She will be greatly missed, said a quote from Mrs. Hastings. She got the last quote, the article over.

CHAPTER
TEN

December

"Holy hell, girl. Finally. How are you? How's LA and what's this number?"

I circulated the area of the payphone I currently broke down and made a call at. I told Birdie I'd call her sometime, just hadn't told her when.

I watched a tumbleweed literally tumble down the street and pressed the phone to my ear. "Good. Things are good, and this is a payphone. My phone charger is still broken."

A half-truth, of course, my phone charger was broken, but I lied about how things were in my life currently. Oh yeah, and the little white lie I told her before about where I was. Keeping up the lie about all that felt best in this situation, though. In all honesty, I trusted Birdie, but telling her anything did put pressure on her. It was just easier to keep things to myself for the time being.

"Oh, awesome," she said. It sounded like she was at a game or something, a lot of activity in the background or maybe practice. She and the other basketball players were currently off season but they had intramurals. "It's good to hear from you. The others have been asking about you. Well, literally everyone is asking about you."

I bet they were, the new girl coming to the school to rescue her sister only for said sister to turn up dead. The rumor and gossip mill had been ridiculous when I'd been there, and now that I actually gave people a valid reason to talk about me? I shook my head. "Yeah?"

"Yeah. You coming back soon? We all miss you over here."

I knew they did, my smile faint. She and the others had become pretty good friends to me in my short time there. We had our drama moments a little bit, but eventually, we'd gotten over it. Things had been good until they weren't. I turned with the phone cord. "Probably not for a while. Things are nice here, you know? Easy?"

I felt all that was self-explanatory, and Birdie agreed with me, her soft "Mmmhmm" into the phone.

"I get it. I do," she said, then stopped. "Well, I don't... You know what I mean."

I pushed my hand through hair that hadn't seen a shower in over twenty hours. I showered at the local YMCA or the homeless shelter, but since I hadn't made it in last night... I gripped my arm. "I do know what you mean."

A pregnant silence filled the line, as awkward as this conversation. I mean, what did we say to each other? I was lying to her, and she didn't know how to deal. There wasn't a manual on how to console a friend when they were literally on the cusp of a breakdown.

Which I was...

"Things with all that, what people were saying before you left is starting to blow over. I'm sure, by the time you come back, it won't be a thing."

I turned with the cord again. All that, a decision I made in another life, was the least of my worries. That happened when you were trying to figure out how to keep food coming when you didn't have a lot.

"So I'm just saying if that's the reason why you're not coming back... If that's why, it'll all blow over. People aren't even really talking about it anymore."

She could be lying herself in an attempt to get me back, but even so, I wasn't buying. That wasn't the reason I wasn't coming back.

It just helped my case.

"It's not," I said. "And I'm sure it will."

"It will." She sounded hopeful, her voice hard to hear with all that going on in the background. "And oh, I almost forgot to mention. Your dad asked about you. Well, talked to my dad who talked to me. My dad cleans up at the building your dad works at, I guess, so they work together kinda."

I froze, not knowing what to say.

"He said he hadn't heard from you?" she stated, allowing the air to release from my lungs a little. "Anyway, he requested if I talked to you to have you reach out. I won't, though, if you don't want me to."

Why Dad even bothered when he didn't care I didn't know. "I'd prefer not. I ghosted him for a reason. I need time to deal with everything."

"Gotcha. I'm sure Royal will be talking to you about it too. I saw him talking to your dad outside the school the other day. I assumed he was asking about you."

"What did Royal say? I mean." I paused, wrestling my hair around. "Did you hear anything?"

"Not really. Want me to ask?"

Asking would only open up more bullshit, and deep down, I really didn't care about what was exchanged between him and my dad. They were both irrelevant to me.

As irrelevant as Maywood Heights.

————

"You know computer usage is limited to one hour, right?"

Beanie Boy no longer wore his beanie, his head a wash of thick curls as dark and umber-toned as his eyes. He looked different today, less get-the-fuck-out-of-my-library and more evening cafe in his acid-wash jeans and dark sweater. He pushed the sleeves up his golden arms. "Just want to make sure you know."

I apparently had a time Nazi on my hands, but I guess I had been here an hour or... four. I supposed I got wrapped up with what I'd been doing.

My nod firm, Beanie Boy finally stopped eyeing me long enough to go back to returning books on the shelves. He reserved judgment for me the moment he noticed my return to the library, and though I didn't blame him considering our first interaction, it still sucked. I wasn't a thief. At least not generally.

Shaking my head, I went back to the computer, planning to wrap things up. I'd been searching news articles about my sister, which led me down a total rabbit hole considering how many there'd been. I'd been surprised by that, my sister's story well traveled. I guess I ignored a lot of those initial publications when they came out. I'd been too raw, too hurt, and though things hadn't gotten much better, I wanted to see my sister's face again. I wanted to see her happy and bright, and that offset some of the, quite frankly, bullshit the media spewed about my sister and what happened on the night in question. They didn't really know what happened, but they sure as hell believed they did. My sister having too much to drink that night turned into a news story about a young teen with drugs in her system and a night of mistakes. Those mistakes had cost her the young life she had, and each publication only spiced the article up more. Some people didn't even have her name right, all of this complete bullshit.

I too still had a lot of questions about that night, questions I hadn't gotten to ask considering I wasn't currently speaking to Royal. I wanted to know more about that girl that set everything off for my sister, and as far as I was concerned, what happened to Paige had been her fault. Paige may have gotten drunk and wandered some train tracks, but this girl had sent her there.

I guess she's irrelevant too.

I couldn't really do anything about her where I was right now, neither physically nor mentally. At the present, I was forced to figuratively let ghosts die, and my chest hurt, pained with every article I continued to read.

"Fucking tragic," came from behind me, the library boy with his unruly hair and familiar sour expression. He kept that strong on me, tipping his chin from where he stood at the bookshelves. He'd been putting books away, his long reach toward the top of a shelf. "That news story? Crazy it made its way all the way here."

"What do you mean?" I pushed back from the computer. He knew about this? What happened to my sister?

On the toes of his Converses, he returned to his feet, tugging down a shirt that revealed a clear sliver of abs. I didn't know why, but that surprised me. Maybe because he was in *here* and not out with the land of the living on a Friday night. He shrugged. "What happened out there went down in my hometown."

What the fuck?

"Your hometown?" I tried to sound aloof, but what were the fucking odds of that happening?

Library boy seemed casual about it, crossing long arms and lounging back against the shelves. He really was tall and didn't even need a step stool to reach to the highest bookshelf. "Yeah. Crazy, right? Can't believe that happened."

"What do you know about it?" Aloof again. I had to be as to not raise suspicion. I didn't know this guy, nor who he knew. Maywood Heights wasn't huge, and we very well could know some of the same people if he was originally from there.

He frowned. "Not much. Just that a girl died on the train tracks. How did you come to know about it? Just searching the web?"

I nodded, his look passive when he bent to pick up more books. He'd been deliberately reshelving them around me on and off in the time I'd been here, and that I knew. He had his eye on me, this boy.

"Anyway, yeah, it was messed up," he said. "Not surprising considering where I lived. People there are on a different level of drama and craziness. Needless to say, I was happy I got out when I did."

I didn't like what he said in regards to my sister, but I couldn't disagree with him about all the drama in Maywood Heights. I'd been the target of enough myself, and I hadn't even been there a full semester.

"Why did you leave?" I asked, and he turned, books in his hands.

"Wasn't really a good fit," he said, frowning again. "Why do you ask?"

"No reason." I passed it off easily, turning around and scanning more articles. The boy didn't move right away behind me, but eventually he moved to the shelves toward the right of me. He placed more books.

"You in school or anything?"

Shit.

I moved my jaw. "Why do you ask?"

A shrug and then a look. "Just wondered. You came in here today when most people who look your age would be at school."

How motherfrickin' observant of him? I clicked aimlessly. "Yeah, I'm in school," I lied, exaggerating what I said to make my school status sound obvious. "You?"

"Mmhmm. College." He placed a book, stopping. "I'm a freshman at the university a town over."

"Awesome," I said, so not awesome. I didn't really care, and he seemed way too about this conversation right now for my liking.

He lingered. "Where do you go?"

This guy…

"Community college," I gritted, daring to face him. "I go to the one here. I'm a freshman too."

I figured this was a safe lie considering he said he went to the university outside of town. What were the odds of him taking a class at the community college if that were the case?

I waited, trying to play off the fact that I very much had damp armpits. I paused for a retort, but when I didn't get one, the boy turning away, I let out a breath.

"Name's Ramses, by the way," he said, gathering a few books off a rolling cart. "You?"

I really didn't want to give this boy my name, but he was totally bugging.

"December," I told him. "And Ramses? Like the pharaoh?"

He smirked, shaking his head when he shelved more books. "Yeah, but I don't know how much of a king I am."

Being a king was highly overrated, any kind of royalty the same as far as I was concerned. He hit a sore spot with me. Though, unbeknownst to him, and when he came over this time, he was book-free.

"Nice to meet you, December," he said, smiling a little. His smile faded. "You got fifteen minutes. You can't be on this thing all day. Sorry."

Fucking Christ. This guy's chill could make ice sculptures, but he at least left me this time so I could have those few minutes. I was finishing up when he came through the back again, but this time from a store room. He had a sign in his hands reading "Help

Wanted," and when I asked him about that he stopped his pace. He lifted it. "The librarian is looking. He lives upstairs and wants some help for days when I'm in classes. Why?"

I didn't necessarily want but needed a job. I needed money, food and working at some place as easygoing as this would definitely help.

"I'm looking for work," I said, standing. I had my mini duffel bag with me, picking it up and placing it over my shoulder. "If he's looking for someone..."

"I don't know," he returned, that familiar eye on me. He tossed an arm against the shelf. "He's looking for someone who can handle responsibility. Someone on the up-and-up who can take care of things around here."

Meaning, he didn't want a thief, and shaking my head, I turned around.

"Never mind," I told him, moving to print off the articles I found, then log off. I was done here and would make sure I used the internet at the cafe from now on. I thought Ramses would move along, go to the front of the store and put up his sign, but he didn't, steps coming slowly toward me.

They stopped. "If that's you, I can put a good word in, though. What day could you start?"

CHAPTER
ELEVEN

December

Come on. Come on. Juice up. Juice up…

The second the dead battery signal faded away made my life, my phone screen lighting up. Immediately, text messages and missed calls started flooding in, and I hunkered down, trying to stay quiet in the library's bathroom. It was just about the only place I could go where Ramses didn't hover, and as he tended to hover *everywhere*, I had to wait until here and this moment to put good use to my first paycheck. I got the cell phone charger as soon as humanly possible, and after obviously feeding myself, I headed down to one of the local banks to cash my paycheck. I'd been working about a week in the library, and it'd been great for the most part. Albeit boring.

I'd choose that over what I came from.

Dragging my thumb across the lock screen, I studied text messages first, Birdie, Kiki, and Shakira, as well as some from Rosanna and, of course, Aunt Celeste. Dad hadn't left any text messages, obviously not his bag, but he'd left enough phone calls to fill my voicemail box to the point of suffocation. He'd probably shut my cell phone off by now, but maybe not if he wanted a means to call me.

I put the phone to my ear, not listening to his voicemails but Aunt Celeste's.

"Please call me," she said about three weeks ago. *"What are you thinking? This isn't like you, and it's scaring me."*

I closed my eyes, going to another.

"December Lindquist, you're putting me through hell right now. Call me. What the hell…"

Her voice had broken up, and before I thought better of it, I called her, hoping to God my dad did shut my cell phone off.

"December? December, thank God!"

He hadn't shut my phone off, my back sliding down the wall until my butt touched the floor. I closed my eyes. "Hi, Aunt C."

"'Hi, Aunt C.,'" she chimed, an exasperated and almost disturbed tone to her voice that gutted me. I hadn't meant to hurt her, just wanted to relieve her. She sounded anything but, breathing hard into the phone. "Are you okay? Where are you?"

I wasn't telling her that, staying silent.

"You're not telling me that," she concluded, my aunt smart. "But at least tell me if you're okay."

"I'm fine. I swear, and I haven't been ignoring you on purpose. My phone died and…"

"Oh, don't give me that, December Lindquist. You could have called. You could have *called* instead of leaving your dad a note and me a cell phone message. Christ."

She didn't normally talk that way, and though she had worked a lot and I pretty much raised myself growing up, she had been there for me. She cared about me, took me in.

I pressed a palm to my eyes. "I just needed space, okay?"

"You needed space." Her tone was dry. "What about me?

What about your dad? December… he didn't know what to think."

This had been the first time in true history my aunt went to bat for my dad—ever—but she was so wrong about what she was saying. My dad didn't care, not really, and those last words I heard him share with her through a thick wall showed me that. I was an obligation just like I had been to her. He didn't know what to do with me, something he'd actually said on, of all days, the worst one of my life. I buried my sister that day. He buried a child, and his first thought was to rid himself of another. You'd think he'd learn after losing my mom *and* sister the value of family.

I squeezed eyes beneath my palm.

"This is something your sister would have done, *did* do," Aunt Celeste said, teary. "Please don't do anything stupid. Please don't—"

"I'm not," I emphasized, true tears now. Fuck, I hadn't managed to cry in weeks. I wiped them away. "I'm safe. I'm doing well. I took a bus out here and I'm fine."

"Took it where? Honey, let me come and get you or at least send for you. Are you close?"

"No, I'm not, and no, I'm not coming back. At least not now, Aunt C., and don't push."

My warning had her silent, a true warning even if I hadn't meant to threaten. My aunt had about two more seconds of this before the call went stale, and I think she knew that.

"Call your dad and call *me* every day, or anytime you need something. Do you have money?"

"I do. I got a job."

"You got a job," she parroted, her voice dry. "A high school dropout."

I hadn't thought about it that way, but I guess I was. My dad had called the school before we left the Midwest for my sister's service, telling them it'd be a little bit before I came back. Something told me running away hadn't been what he had in mind when he originally made the call, though.

I dampened my lips. "Goodbye, Aunt C."

"Goodbye? December, wait—"

I clicked off before I could get more emotional, rising from my bottom. I went to the mirror, and a little flushed, I washed the tears away from a face filled with color. I'd gotten a good shower this morning, so at least my hair looked decent, up and out of my face. Ramses also didn't seem to mind the nose piercing, so that stayed too. After getting in a few breaths, I threw the paper towel away I used to dry my face, then clicked off the light in the bathroom, closing the door. Ramses was at the front when I came out, dark eyes flicking up from the computer.

"Everything go all right in there?" he asked, a little less chilly now that he knew I had no intent to rob the library blind. I never saw, but I was sure he took inventory of each and every one of the articles here after my first couple shifts.

I smirked a little. "Did you seriously just ask me if it went okay in the bathroom?"

Overly bushy eyebrows shot up like he just became aware of what he'd both asked and said. I mean, his eyebrows weren't overgrown but they were definitely thick like his curly hair. He scrubbed in the curls. "Never mind. Forget I asked."

Happy to laugh, I did let it go, *Ramses* not a foreign thing to me anymore. Something told me he never planned to actually talk to anyone around this place, let alone work with someone else. We rarely got people coming through here, and when we did, he completely filled their ear with nerd speak. He quite literally knew everything about all the stuff on the shelves here, even out-talking the librarian, Myron, who I met my first official day as staff. The older man kept to himself for the most part, staying upstairs unless needed, and with someone like Ramses managing the library a hell of a lot of the time, that wasn't much.

All that awkwardness with us out of the way, Ramses logged off the front computer, then reached back to the coat rack behind the desk. He grabbed a jacket there, suede and nice.

"You just about ready to lock up?" he asked, slipping it on. "I can walk you home if need be since it's getting late."

He'd picked up on the fact that I didn't have a car the first day when he caught me walking down the street, so it was easy for him to assume I either lived nearby or took public transport. Either way, I wasn't off the hook when it came to explanation. He *did* have a car, so even if I claimed I didn't live close and attempted to take public transpiration he'd probably try to drive me someplace to be nice.

Fucking chivalry.

It was seriously biting me in the ass right now. I'd given him a fake address I'd Googled on the library computers, and he obviously hadn't looked into it. If he did, he'd know I gave him a pretty crappy residence in what looked like an abandoned neighborhood on Google Street View.

"Actually, I was wondering if I could stay and lock up," I asked, not about to tell this guy I was homeless. He might judge me like he initially had, my new job already gone. I shrugged. "I have some cataloging I wanted to finish, and I don't mind staying. You don't even have to pay me for the extra time."

This might have been laying it on a little thick, but I was desperate here, Ramses' look curious when he turned with his keys.

Thick eyebrows drew inward. "I don't know. I mean, that's not a *big* deal, but it kinda is. You've never done that before, and it's only been a week since you started here."

He had no reason to trust me really. I hadn't given him

any reason at all except the week I had spent here working with him.

He came forward with his keys. "If you think you can handle it?"

If the alternative was him trying to get me home... yeah, I could handle it. I didn't want to lose my job if he didn't like that I had no place to go. "Yeah. Totally can. Give me a chance?"

I put my lip out for emphasis, and rolling his eyes, he eventually gave me keys. They felt heavy in my hands, but good. I wanted him to trust me. I could do this.

"I'm letting Myron know you're down here, though," he said, eyeing me. "I'm gonna text him after I leave, and make sure you follow the checklist he has for close up. He hates when you, well, anyone veers off it."

I saluted. "Aye, aye, Captain."

He smirked, his chuckle light as he zipped up his coat. I intended to make him laugh, so I guess mission accomplished. He pointed at me. "I'm putting faith in you. My rep's on the line here."

Him saying that made my smile fade for some reason. It reminded me of someone else, someone in another life and time who'd also put their neck out for me. According to him, it'd been repeatedly.

According to me it'd been repeatedly too.

It didn't make up for how things ended, though, and swallowing, I nodded at Ramses. He grabbed his bag, sliding it over his chest. "Night, December."

"Night."

Backing away, he turned over the "Open" sign, the door chiming when he went out. He waited for me to lock it before he left, and I peeked through the blinds to watch him head over to a more than nice ride. Parked across the street, the sleek Mercedes could turn anyone's head and definitely wasn't the typical college student's car. If anything, someone in Maywood Heights would be driving something like that at his age.

He must be loaded too. Everyone else in that town was.

Flicking the blinds, I put my hands on my hips. I actually had no cataloging to do, just wanted to kill some time and get Ramses off me for a second. He could be terribly nosy, but things with us had gotten better in the last week, easier. Still figuring I had to prove myself, I decided to clean up around the library for as long as I could before doing Myron's check-list. This didn't take a whole lot of time, as Ramses was meticulous about cleaning too, and after shaking my head at him for that, I called it an evening. I found my bag in the store room, the place I usually kept it during a shift. I tried to keep it out of eyesight for the most part, since it was cumbersome and not the typical-sized bag a girl would carry. Ramses had seen it before, but I made sure not beyond that day I asked about the library needing help.

Taking it, I ventured over to the children's section. They had a lot of pillows in there for the kids, and I used them, tossing my bag down. I pushed it all together and made a little lying area for myself, setting my phone timer before folding my arms over my chest and closing my eyes. I'd only sleep for a couple hours, max. Myron would most likely be down here to check on things eventually, check that I'd made it out okay and locked up, and anyway, I wasn't trying to take advantage of the situation or the fact Ramses put trust in me to close. I'd leave here tonight, make sure everything was good, and then, I'd head back to where I was supposed to be, under the bridge my sleeping place tonight. I was grateful for the job I'd gotten and those who'd given it to me, truly...

I just wanted some sleep behind a locked door for once.

CHAPTER
TWELVE

December

A few days later, I scrolled through social media at a local park for what felt like the first time in forever, and it sorta had been, I guess. I'd had computer access, but when I did, I wasn't looking into my past and what the world was doing without me.

It seemed they were doing just fine.

My applications showed me people were doing pretty hella frickin' awesome: Birdie, Kiki, and the others at games and taking selfies at the mall. I saw people smiling and getting on just cool without me, the new girl with a dead sister. Even my aunt had posted a few things during her rounds at the hospital, people clearly forcing her into hugs, but she'd participated.

Christ.

My heart stopped, literally stopped, at seeing Royal Prinze. It'd been awhile. It hadn't been long enough, and that breath had nowhere to go when I saw him with friends, one in particular.

He had his arm around... *Mira*, the bitch Mira, at some kind of party. She had a drink in her hand, they both did, and though it could have meant nothing, it had before. It probably did. She'd come to my sister's reception. They both had pretty much been together then, and only after he left her had he found me.

Is that why he didn't come with me?

I wouldn't let my thoughts go there. I truly couldn't let my thoughts go down that road because if I did, there'd be no coming back. No, my sister's best friend hadn't ditched her memorial service to cater to Mira, and no, he hadn't abandoned me to be with her too. I refused to believe it.

I studied the photo again, the boy too beautiful for his own goddamn good. He was still completely gorgeous, willowy blond locks he had styled and feathered and a body so thick and hard I could still feel it pressed against my skin. I could still feel *him*, deep and full within me. He didn't look like he was sad or even grieving. He looked like he was moving on, and he'd done so clearly without me.

I removed myself from his friend list and follower accounts, blocking him wherever I could, and got so into it I scared myself. I came at this task with a vengeance, my insides burning and raw.

"December?"

Jumping, I gazed up, my eyes widening at the sight of Ramses... with friends. Well, not that he had friends per se, but because of what they all wore.

Uniforms. Like legit *academy* uniforms donned him and the two friends he'd brought at his sides. They looked like Royal... Royal and Court. Especially Ramses as he had a tie loosened over a pearl white dress shirt, his eyes equally wide on me.

My lips parted. "Um, hi."

"Hey." Ramses pushed two long fingers behind his neck, scratching aimlessly. Clearly caught, he stood there with the rest of his uniformed brethren. The boy had told me he was in college, but those outfits were anything but, the colors of green and flame yellow making its way through the whole thing from the ties to the crests on their jackets. They also had cups of ice cream in their hands, the spoon in the mouth of the guy on the right and the one on the left exchanging a glance between Ramses and me. Ramses stopped eating his period, blinking out of whatever daze he'd been in to face his friends. "Guys, this is December," he said, clearly forgetting himself. "We work together at the library."

We exchanged our customary "hey there" and "hello," but after I'd fallen out of the stupor *I'd* been in, I put my phone away and stood from the bench. I eyed Ramses. "You told me you were in college."

He started to speak, but stopped. He cleared this throat. "Eh, uh. You told me the same."

Shit.

I had said that, and when we both realized the bullshit we gave each other, *trying to play* the other, we both had a laugh at our own expenses. Ramses shrugged broad shoulders. "We skip all the time. I'd rather be making money than going to sleep in class. We go to an academy over in Crestfire Hills."

Aware of the city a town over, I nodded, and Ramses' more burly friend, the one the size of a mini monster truck, threw a fist into Ramses' shoulder.

"*He* skips to work. We skip for froyo!" Backing up, the mini-monster-truck friend bumped chests with the literal monster-truck-sized friend to Ramses' right, the two completely bros and the opposite of Ramses. Dare I say, I thought he was a little bit of a nerd, but seeing him with his friends, I might have been wrong with the assumption.

Ramses knocked the two on their heads for being idiots, making me genuinely laugh in what felt like had been a while. A good belly laugh I think I needed, but all that stopped at least for Ramses when his friend directed a froyo cup my way and asked a question.

"You should hang out with us," the mini-monster-truck friend said, puffing up. "We're going to a college party—"

"I'm sure she's busy." Ramses cut that off quick, so quick my head nearly spun. He faced me. "You're busy, right? Tell them you're busy."

I wasn't, and I really didn't like he thought he could speak for me. Actually, him not wanting me to go out with him and his friends made me want to hang out with them more. Call that me being cheeky.

I smiled. "I'm totally free actually," I said, genuinely happy for the invite. It'd be nice to do something besides basically stalk my ex all day. I started to go with the guys, but Ramses held me back a little.

He gazed over my shoulder. "You forgot your bag," he said, lowering his hand and calling attention to my stuff. "Wouldn't want to forgot that."

I didn't know what he meant by that, but I held back and grabbed it. I was sure knowing Ramses I'd find out. He was always one to speak his mind after all, at least when it came to me.

CHAPTER
THIRTEEN

December

The guys *de*-academied themselves in Ramses' Mercedes Benz, removing jackets and pushing up shirt sleeves to "blend in" once we got to the party. Crestfire Hills turned out to be more than an hour away, and since I had worked with Ramses, I trusted these guys not to murder me—for the most part. Ramses was definitely aware of me in the passenger seat, but I think mostly because of his friends. They were complete jocks. Seriously, the way they talked about sports, video games, and *girls*... needless to say, I heard it all and laughed through most of it. Being with them all reminded me of better and normal times, though I hated to admit that. The car trip reminded me of homecoming night, the moments before things got shitty and my life had been kinda all right. In actuality, the strange comfort of the feeling triggered something that had me putting distance between them and myself the moment we did get to the party. It was in some kind of frat house on campus, the "welcome" sign making the event out to be some kind of open house. Bodies mingled and drank, drank and mingled like a typical college social gathering. I attempted to move away from the party I arrived with in the influx of it, but I noticed Ramses stayed close. He looked out for me, even going first so I could walk and stuff through the crowd, and I didn't know if it was because he felt he had to (maybe since he took his sole, *female* coworker more than an hour away), but whatever compelled the boy in half an academy uniform to take care of me tonight. He actually looked kind of in his element here, his tie and academy jacket gone and his dress shirt untucked. He left all that and who he was in the car, standing before me kinda *thicc* with the surprising amount of muscular definition he usually kept stashed away behind chunky sweaters of various designs. He definitely wasn't a nerd. At least a weak one. He looked at me. "So this is a college party."

Laughing, I nodded. "Apparently."

His eyes smiled more than his mouth, but not in a bad way. He'd never been one to be flagrant about being happy. I could tell he wanted to sometimes, but was obviously very cautious about me and what to make of me. At least, that's what I assumed. Again, I'd given him a reason to be hesitant about me so I didn't blame him for all that. Through the party people, we made our way to the kitchen, and when Ramses grabbed some red Solo cups off the platter of many for us, I eyed it. "You really trust that?"

Obviously thinking better of it, he cringed before tossing them both and filling us fresh cups from a nearby keg. He gave me one, and by the time he filled another, I'd already drunk mine. I handed him back the cup, awesome at drinking. I shook for another, and his eyes bugged the hell out.

"Whoa there, tiger. Save some for the fishes," he said, though he poured me mine. He handed it to me.

"Fishes don't drink," I told him, getting a big ole gulp. I waved it for him to top me off, and raising his thick, dark eyebrows, he did.

"True. Though you should probably take it a little easy," he said.

He wasn't in charge of me, but since I'd gotten myself into trouble the last time I heavily drank, I didn't fill my cup any more after taking another sip. I gestured toward his cup. "You just going to nurse that or let me make a fool of you?"

His pride clearly at stake, Ramses lifted his cup but made a point to shake his head first before taking a swallow. Joining him, we did so together, but I didn't guzzle down what I had this time. We ended up taking our drinks as we walked through the house and came across one of his friends, the mini-monster-truck-sized one who looked a little like Chris Pratt if I squinted. I mean, I had to squint really hard but I could see it. Anyway, the dude was totally under another keg, sucking down booze while a couple of shirtless guys with spirit paint on their chests chanted him on.

Ramses tucked a hand under his armpit, shaking his head. "Can't take him anywhere."

"Obviously," I said, smiling a little before taking a drink. I noticed Ramses' more than familiar *eye* on me, and I lowered my arm. "What?"

His doe-colored eyes narrowed a little, his look curious when he tilted his head. "What's your deal anyway?"

"Deal?"

"Yeah. You weren't in school today."

"You weren't either."

"I had a reason. School and all that's basically bullshit for me. I get ahead super fast and really just spend the time sleeping. Senior year has especially been a joke. I'm ahead like three credits but I have to go to graduate."

Jesus. He was smart, a nerd albeit an unconventional one.

I wished my reasons for skipping class had been the same as his, but because they weren't I either had to lie again or come up with some fraction of the truth to give him.

"I was in school, but I'm not now," I said, choosing the

truth. I shrugged. "Don't need it in the place I'm at in my life right now."

"Which is?" he asked, then pointed toward my arm. "And what's with the bag? You carrying your life in there or something?"

Damn, I knew I should have left this thing in the car.

It was instinctual not to, someone could take it from me. All I had. I adjusted it. "I'm not in school because I don't want to be. Happy?"

"Not really," he confessed, taking another sip of booze. "Just more curious."

I had my own curiosity when it came to him. I pointed at him now. "What about you?"

"What about me?"

"It's one thing for you to leave a town… that one you said you came from because of college, but it's entirely another to just up and leave in high school—which you obviously were in." I tried to sound passive about it, shrugging. "What really happened there? Why did you leave?"

I wondered if he'd actually tell me. I wondered if I overstepped and that may direct more questions at me, which I didn't need. Ramses' frown wasn't small, and when he threw an arm against the wall, he didn't look at me.

"There was a clique there."

My heart squeezed.

"Had a run-in with them," he stated, deadpan. The drink he took had him sucking his teeth after. "Anyway, after I voiced my opinions about it, my dad gratefully shipped me off to boarding school so he wouldn't have to deal with my objections about it. That worked out just fine with me. I flipped that place and that school the bird. Never looked back since."

So his dad was into the Court and he wasn't. That's assuming we went to the same school…

What were the odds?

It all made sense, though. Ramses clearly had some kind of money and being able to be shipped off to boarding school in the first place made that pretty much a given. We came from the same place, had similar "run-ins," and his dad got rid of him.

I chewed my lip. "My dad can be kind of a jerk too."

His gaze slid over, his arm dropping from the wall. "He's okay with you just not being in school?"

"Hardly." I laughed, staring off. "He basically disowned me."

"So you're on your own?"

My eyes flashed, this guy way too intuitive.

He smiled a little. "Just a theory."

Well, he'd be too right and enough for me not to want to continue this conversation.

"Maybe where I was in life happens to be just as shit as where you were in yours," I gave him, the two of us more in sync than he could possibly imagine. I mean, we were literally from the same town, those odds truly astronomical, but they happened.

He stared down at me. "I hope you're wrong about that."

"Why?"

"Because no one deserves that." A lengthy finger tapped his cup before he smiled a little. "Not even a dirty little thief like yourself."

My jaw dropped, the guy completely busting out in laughter. I smacked his arm. "What the fuck?"

"Relax. I know you didn't steal anything from Myron or the library," he said, easing away when I tried to hit him again. "I've been watching you."

My lips closed, but before I could say anything about that, the pair of us noticed a shuffle up front. It all surrounded two officers, two *police* officers, making their way through the crowd, and when they started questioning people, Ramses took my drink from me.

He put his and mine on an end table. "That's our cue. Come on. We need to find the guys. Wouldn't want to add to that rap sheet of yours."

His comment was only left on the floor due to the strict fear I didn't want to get arrested for underage drinking tonight. Ramses obviously felt the same because he had us bolting in quick time amongst more than a few people flooding out the house with us. We weren't the only ones probably drinking when we shouldn't be. Ramses and I sprinted outside, but we didn't see his friends. We ended up down the street and in his car by ourselves, but after a couple quick texts, Ramses started his car.

"The guys are headed to another party with some others," he said, turning in his leather seats. "Want to go?"

With it getting even later, I probably shouldn't. Heading back was quite a drive, and I didn't want to be put out of the shelter again tonight by getting back too late. I was also kind of buzzed and probably shouldn't be drinking any more anyway. I asked Ramses if he could take me home, and after confirming with his friends they'd take ride shares back, he said he would. He asked for my address and the one I made up before was on my lips before I could think better of it.

I hoped to God no one actually lives there.

That was my only thought as Ramses drove me more than an hour it took to get back to town. It was dark then, deeply dark, and my anxiety only skyrocketed the closer he got to my made-up address. We ended up pulling into a cul-de-sac that barely had streetlamps working, Google Maps definitely accurate. The neighborhood looked completely abandoned and the house Ramses pulled us to a stop in front of the same. There were boards on the windows and everything, no lights on and the gate at the front broken.

"Are you sure this is the right place?" he asked, leaning over the steering wheel. He sat back. "The whole neighborhood looks kinda… sketchy."

Probably because it was, but I said nothing. I started to go, but stopped when he unbuckled himself. "What are you doing?"

He stopped too. "Was going to walk you up? Seriously, this place looks rough. I mean, I don't mean to insult where you live—"

"Then don't," I shot, making his eyes widen. I was just tired of his fucking chivalry and shit, his meddling. I opened the door. "I'm fine."

"December…"

His hand on my arm, I ripped it away.

He put his up. "I just don't think this feels right."

"I told you. I'm fine—"

"You don't live here," he rushed, immediately making my lips clamp tight. He wrestled with curls. "At least I don't think you do. It seems like you don't. Like you don't *live* anywhere really."

I said nothing, my heart racing, and he lowered his hand.

"You carry a shit-ton of stuff with you everywhere." He tossed a hand to the bag at my feet, sighing. "Then there's that conversation you were having in the bathroom…"

"You were spying on me?" Heated now, *livid.* "That was private."

"I know. I know and I'm sorry, but I'm concerned. You're obviously on your own and Myron… Myron caught you sleeping at the library the other day."

My body shook, my lips quivering open. "I left. I didn't stay."

"No. Yes. I know, but that's not the point—"

"The point, *Ramses*, is that you need to mind your own goddamn business and stay the hell out of mine."

"December."

Getting my bag, I opened the door, basically shutting it in his face. I pointed at him through glass. "Go. Go and get the fuck out of here. I don't need you or your help."

I pushed off the door and when he started to follow me down the street with his car I turned, flipping him off.

He stopped then, his hands on the wheel. He didn't move, just… stared at me, judging me like he did that first day. "I want to help," he mouthed through the windshield, but I didn't want his help.

I pointed again. "Then go."

He sat there with that, stark still, but eventually, he raised his hands. He put the car in gear with what appeared to be a sigh, pulling off from the side of the road and making a U-turn. His sleek Mercedes cruised down the street, and I closed my eyes.

Could you be nastier to him?

Knowing that he had just wanted to help, I put palms to my forehead and walked away. I had no idea how at all I'd deal with that at work or even if I had a job anymore.

Myron knows I slept there…

I kept messing up, doing stupid things, and I fought tears, trying to figure out how the fuck I was going to get to the shelter from wherever I was at. Pulling out my cell phone, I decided to figure that latter part out, and my heart sank to the depths even more. I was far enough away that I wouldn't be able to walk there before the shelter's doors closed for the night. They had a strict "no-entrance" policy after a certain hour, and I definitely wasn't going to make it.

Stopping in the middle of the sidewalk, I decided to pony up the money for a ride share, thinking it'd be worth it when I started walking down the street.

Especially when a car came out of nowhere.

It went slow down the street, the lights off and in my periphery. Rather than stare at it and the driver, I cut through the alley, probably not the best idea, but when I pushed into the shadows the car kept driving on, a dark SUV.

You're frickin' paranoid, girl.

And a little buzzed. Not to mention emotional. My head

woozy, I decided to continue down the alley to the other street, almost crashing into someone the moment I found sidewalk.

The man's eyes widened, a couple men drinking beneath a streetlamp, but the one to the right I recognized.

He recognized me too, coming forward with a bottle poking out of a brown bag, and the moment he realized where from, he pointed at me. "You're the bitch who stole from my store."

Fuck.

I backed up, then ran the moment he grabbed for me. He missed.

His friend hadn't.

He grabbed me, strong-arming me as I heard something horrible fall from the shop guy's lips.

"Hold her down," he said, throwing his beer bottle to the street. It crashed into a million tiny pieces under the street-light, the shop guy messing with his pants. "We'll show her not to steal from me."

I screamed, my voice stifled when a hand came over my mouth. Shop guy did that while he messed with his pants, trying to get his junk out, but a car screeching to a stop not only made him hesitate but run when a force the size of a young gorilla came charging out of the car like a beast out of a cave. That force grabbed the shop guy, throwing him down, and the beast sent a blow into his face.

The blows didn't stop. They came hit after charging hit, as this huge guy literally pummeled the shop dude's face in. His hand came away bloody, the guy looking back at me and shouting for me to get into his car.

I got a good look at his face then, his voice chilling and dragging me right back into my past. Knight Reed was beating a dude's face in.

Knight Reed was killing a guy for me.

CHAPTER
FOURTEEN

December

"Knight… stop!" I physically had to pull him off the guy, no easy feat with his size and strength. In the end, I think he submitted only because he didn't want to swing back and accidentally hit me, my tiny hands on his arm as I dragged him away. He caught a look at the shop guy's friend on the way and when he went for him next I had to pull harder.

The friend ran like the chickenshit he was, the guy not knowing how close to death he was if I let go of this boy.

What the hell?

"Knight, what are you doing here—"

"Get in the damn car, December," he grunted, physically tossing another man's blood into the street when he flicked his hand. His next venture apparently consisted of getting my bag because he spun, picking it, then grabbed *me* by the arm on the way back. He opened the SUV's door, tossed the bag in the back, and after forcing my stunned body inside, got into the car himself.

He peeled away like the psycho he was, the guy he

pummeled rolling to his front in the side-view mirror. I only let out a breath when I noticed him get up, but I didn't get a look long before Knight rounded a corner like he didn't know what brakes were.

"What the fuck are you doing here?" I shot, bumping around and trying to get my seat belt on. Knight pulled another tight corner and I had to grab the dash. "Slow *down*. How did you even find me anyway?"

So many questions in his car, but none of them he seemed to want to answer. On top of his fierce driving, he grabbed his phone, texting something before tossing it in the cup holder. This was obviously a rented car, something I didn't recognize.

"If you didn't want someone finding you, probably shouldn't have posted a tagged photo of where you were on social media," he grunted again, and calling his bullshit, I pulled out my phone. I didn't post anything on social media.

Shit.

I had, a picture I snapped at the park today but I hadn't posted it. At least, I hadn't meant to do so. The picture also tagged itself, hence my "knight" in shining armor here today.

Knight snorted, bull-like in the way he did it. He was amped the hell up and didn't look like he was coming down from that anytime soon. He braced the wheel. "I was already in town when you posted that. Went to that park, and when I didn't find you, I drove around a bit, got lucky when I spotted you at a streetlight a ways back. I followed you after whoever dropped you off."

I swallowed. "Why? And why are you here?"

"Royal."

"Royal?"

He nodded. "He sent me to check on your ass, and thank God I did. I mean, what the fuck did you think you were doing? Buzzed the fuck to hell? You smell like a damn brewery."

Okay, so it was so not that serious. I only had like a couple of drinks and Royal sent him? What the fuck?

"Why the fuck would Royal send you to check on me? Royal doesn't care. He left me, shipped my ass here."

This had him chuckling, but not jovially. He was still pissed, and when I realized he was pulling us onto the highway at basically warp speed, I shot around in my chair. "Where are you taking me?"

"The airport," he said simply like that was cool. "You obviously can't take care of yourself. You're coming home."

"No, you're not!" I started to unbuckle myself, but he was going too fast. "I'm not going home. That's *your* home, not mine—"

"No arguments, December. You're going home. Royal sent me to check on you. I did and I'm making a call."

"Well, you don't have one to make," I said, working my seat belt off. I didn't care how fast we were going. "You're not taking me anywhere. You can't. That's kidnapping."

"Kidnapping or not, I'm doing it," he explained, and when he came to a quick stop, I nearly shot through the window. He lifted up his phone. "Or do you want me to call your dad? Tell him where you are and what almost just happened to you?"

My heart raced. "You wouldn't."

"Wouldn't I?" he stated, starting to dial, and I grabbed his phone.

"Why are you doing this? Why do you even care?" Why did either of them? They hadn't before. They hadn't at all and clearly moved on, him too judging by the pics with Royal. I'd been gone for almost a month.

Knight dampened his lips, pushing fingers through dark strands. "Because Royal asked me to, and Royal is my bro. Your sister was one of those too, and Royal, *Royal and us guys* look out for you. 'Nuff said."

I stared at him, jaw slack in my seat. This had been the

most verbose I'd ever seen him, and for whatever reason, that had me giving him back his phone.

He pocketed it. "Put your seat belt on. I'll drive better. I promise."

Trusting him, I clicked it back on, settling in my seat. He had my hands pretty much tied here.

So long, Arizona.

CHAPTER
FIFTEEN

December

I managed to get a text out to Ramses on the way to the airport. Knight and I were taking a red-eye back to Maywood Heights, and I didn't want him to worry when I didn't show up at work the next day. I also wanted to apologize, and since I wouldn't be coming back, I felt I owed him that. He had been nice, and I'd been shit, letting him know that. I couldn't tell him much, but what I could tell him was that I was going home, and I appreciated everything he did for me. I also told him not to worry and that I was fine, but after that, I shut my phone off. I couldn't take any texts or calls in the air anyway and didn't want to have to deal with anymore explanations. All that done, I continued on with the evening, Knight grabbing my bag and escorting me into the airport. He was a dutiful lackey, seeing through commands by a boy I really was trying hella hard to understand at this point. Royal had said his piece in bounds the moment he put me on a bus and decided not to go with me. Hell, he'd said it before when he didn't go to my sister's memorial and showed up with Mira at the reception. And then those pictures with her?

I sat with all that to myself on a dark plane, a sleeping Knight beside me. He snored to hell, his big body tight on the outer seat, so I couldn't get around him even if I tried. I had no idea what would happen once this plane touched tarmac. But I had a feeling whatever that was wasn't up to me.

I awoke myself to sunlight, low and barely dawn. The flight returning to ground had been easy and after getting my carry-on, Knight was taking us to his car. His Escalade was parked in the lot covered in ice, ready and waiting for the errand boy to come back. I remembered snow before I left Maywood Heights, but actually seeing it in full wintry bursts had been surprising. The trees were lined with it, the air filled with it. The world had changed so much since I'd been gone, and I hadn't been prepared for it.

Knight was, and when he pulled up his car to retrieve both me and my bag, he had a coat with him. He wore it, pulling it off, and after, he gave it to me. "Come on. I don't have two. So…"

He was giving his to me, literally the coat off his back. Not a fool enough to question, I took it, the thing incredibly warm when I put it on. It even smelled like him. Not nearly as good as Royal Prinze, but it did give me a comfort I hadn't expected. I zipped the puffer coat to the top, putting the hood on, and the pair of us got into his ride.

"I'm not going home," I told him, strapping myself in. I shook my head. "I mean, I'm not going to my dad's house." That wasn't home, not anymore.

"You'd be right," he said, pulling away from the curb. He barely flinched at the cold air in the car, obviously used to all this. "You're going to Windsor House."

Windsor House…

I sat low in my seat, at least where we were going was not my house. This held another possibility, and despite remaining silent about his choice of destination, a deep unease brewed in my belly. If we were going to Windsor House, we were quite literally going on Court territory. If we were going to Windsor House, we'd most assuredly be seeing Royal.

I dampened my lips, staring outside at the bare trees and limbs covered in ice. There were several inches of snow on the ground, a familiar town gone, and I sank into the chill. My destiny was as out of my control as it had been when I left, and I let Knight take me through streets I didn't want to be on. I stayed silent all the way to Windsor House, all this ironically familiar. He'd taken me here himself the first time. The lawn had been filled over with Court boys then, guys playing Frisbee under trees that changed colors and a ground full of green. All that was long gone now, and since it was so late— well, early—absolutely no one was out but a groundskeeper past the wrought-iron gates. He waved at Knight when he passed by, allowing us to go up the cobblestone walk to what was basically a castle. Windsor House literally came out of a storybook, in this case the most tragic one for me. I really didn't want to be here, and that showed the minute Knight pulled to the House and I did nothing.

After shutting off the car, he hopped out, coming around to me. He opened the door, and I only unstrapped and got out because it was damn cold and I wanted to get inside. He grabbed my bag, directing us to go through another familiar door. I'd been told once upon a time I'd been the only girl in this section of Windsor House. They hadn't even had my sister back there, and I could only assume because Paige hadn't wanted any part of that and the boys' Court. Or maybe she did but simply wasn't allowed. For whatever reason, they were continuing to make exceptions for me, and I let out a breath once inside only because this time it was empty and not full of judgy stares from boys. It was still too early yet. I guess.

Knight was on his cell phone once inside, typing something on his phone, and I pulled off the coat, a roaring fire nearby.

"Three. Two. One," Knight counted down beside me, and barely after that last word, we weren't alone. Royal stormed in, eyes wild and hair strewn. He looked like he just hopped out of bed.

And fuck did he look hot.

He wore a robe like some ancient goddamn prince, the thing open and displaying his abs as he slapped bare feet to polished tiles. He looked pissed, his cell phone in his hands, and at the sight of me, he stopped completely.

We stared at each other, a beautiful boy and me. I had no idea how I looked, but I knew I hadn't showered in at least twenty-four hours. I was also coming down off a late-ass flight and the drinks I took down before that.

Oh yeah, and the fact that I was nearly assaulted.

Frankly, I probably looked pretty fucking fucked up, and for whatever reason... despite everything and all that happened between us, I wanted him to forget all that. I wanted *me* to forget all that and just let him come to me. I wanted him to hold me, kiss me.

He didn't, his starkly green eyes cutting over to Knight.

"You were supposed to check on her, *not* bring her here," Royal gritted, inserting and twisting the metaphorical dagger deep in my belly. What's worse was it'd felt like he had taken that dagger and stabbed even higher, lodging and slashing across my insides and beating heart. He approached Knight, *not* me. He raised a finger. "She can't be here."

Fuck.

The sensation seared worse, my swallow hard.

"I had no choice," Knight said, then panned to me. "I texted you what happened to her."

He texted him...

He must have, that look between both of them. Especially

Royal. Wild eyes accompanied cheeks filled with blazing red. Like he cared, cared about me.

Royal folded big arms. "There are other places she could have gone."

Smirking with clouded eyes, I gazed away, hating myself for thinking for an absolute moment he did actually care. What happened to him? Him and me? He had cared. At least I thought he had.

Maybe it'd been the abortion or something else. I didn't know, but I stayed silent. The only thing I could do to keep from crying.

"Really, Royal? Please, tell me where, then," Knight continued as if I wasn't there. "Should I have brought her to my house? Yours? You know none of us have been staying at our houses lately."

Lately? They'd been living here? I wondered why, but again stayed quiet.

"Here was the best place," Knight concluded. "We're all here."

They were all here. I guess LJ and Jax somewhere too. I supposed they weren't in on this little coup, then, just these guys.

His hand bunching in his golden locks, Royal appeared conflicted. "Find her a room. We'll figure it out, I guess—"

"Does anyone want to stop talking about me like I'm not standing here?"

I was tired of all this, their male goddamn privilege. They were pushing me around and I'd fucking had it. My jaw worked. "I don't want to stay here and I don't appreciate being *made* to stay here and brought here like some, like some…"

"Someone who can't take care of themselves?" The words had been for me, and only too harsh when they came from Royal. They'd been the first words he'd said to me since the last time we'd been together, that last kiss. His head fell, the shake slight. "Because honestly, December, that's kind of how it sounded. Had Knight not come... Had you been hurt—"

"Don't act like you care," I shot, backing away from whatever *that* was. This boy was playing with me, continuing to play and I was done. I pointed. "And I *can* take care of myself. I have friends. Friends that aren't you."

Sandy-blond hair lifted, his eyes narrowing. His throat jumped. "Fine, then. Figure it out yourself."

I would. I would and I didn't need him.

So why had my heart jumped when he backed away? It was like my tether to him was failing, unraveling quicker than I was ready for, and I hated that. I *hated* that I didn't want to let him go.

He turned. "But you're welcome to stay here until you figure out what you want to do."

I nodded, Knight's coat bunching under my arms. Royal left, and with a nod, Knight gestured me to follow his own exit. I headed behind him, staying at Windsor House for at least one night.

CHAPTER
SIXTEEN

December

"Oh my gosh, December. It's so good to see you!"

Birdie and I embraced outside the gates of Windsor House the next day, pretty early as I wasn't trying to run into any Court boys. I also didn't know if she was actually allowed inside Windsor House, so instead of potentially opening up that can of worms and further risking the wrath of Royal and Knight, I met her there. We took a walk under icicle-covered trees, circulating the property, and since I still had Knight's puffer coat on loan, I took full advantage.

"I still can't believe you were in Arizona this whole time. I mean, what the fuck?" The basketball player joined me on a park bench, breath in small puffs and her cheeks rosy. She shook her head. "Why didn't you tell me?"

My hands deep in Knight's coat, I shook my own head. "I wasn't in a good place." Still wasn't and possibly would never be. I'd been on overdrive since my sister's death, one thing and then the other. I'd never really gotten to mourn her even, all these things crashing down on me. "It's been rough. I was homeless for a little while."

Her eyes bugged out. "Homeless?"

"Yeah." I nodded. "I think what happened to my sister just really messed with my dad. I thought I'd go to live with my aunt in LA, but overhead them both talking about what a burden I was the day of my sister's memorial."

"Shit."

"Mmhmm. It's just been one thing after another."

"So how did you come to be here?" she asked, lifting her head of big dark curls. She had them loose today, flurries from the trees sprinkling down on them. It wasn't snowing, but the snow falling off the trees gave the illusion.

I swallowed. "Knight Reed. I guess Royal sent him down to check on me. They have this... *thing* where they feel like they need to take care of me. Because of Paige, you know? Anyway, whatever about it."

She looked like she understood that, gazing back at Windsor House in the distance. "Well, that's good, I guess. Freaky but good. How was it in there?"

An honest question, but seeing as how I didn't want to answer it, I shrugged. "I just want out. It's too much."

She clasped gloves, staring at me. "Well, of course I'll ask if you can stay with me," she said, the reason I called her. Only a few words of that came out over the phone before she said she wanted to meet me, the reason we were here now. She put a hand on my arm. "And it shouldn't be a problem. Shakira stayed with me for over a month last year when her parents had been fighting. My dad should be cool with it."

I knew she came from a single-parent household, something she'd mentioned in passing. Things were just her and her dad, and that sounded a far cry better than another day spent at Windsor House. Scared to even move, I basically stayed put in the tower Knight had put me in. I hadn't even needed food, all that brought to me and left outside my door. It'd been vegan and everything.

Trying to forget the only person in that place who could have known to do that, I dug my arms deeper in the puffer coat. "And please don't tell anyone I'm here. I really don't want to talk to my dad." He wouldn't be able to do anything. I was eighteen, but I didn't want to deal with him.

She frowned. "Are you not coming back to school? Things really have blown over with..." She didn't say it, but she didn't have to.

"I'm not ashamed about my past, Birdie," I admitted. "There's a reason I did what I did. I was young, but I don't regret it. There was this guy. Took advantage of me my freshman year. I thought I was in love, and when it all went south, well, I did what I had to do, but don't regret it."

She smiled at me. "You're so brave. Stronger than me."

The words chilled, all that said to me before. Paige had said the same thing to me once upon a time.

My heart hurt, dying inside, and though Birdie squeezing my hand helped, the feeling didn't alleviate.

"And of course I won't tell anyone," she said. "I'll see what I can do about you staying with me. I can't imagine living under the Court *eye* would be fun."

She definitely knew my plight, and if she could help me, I'd take it. I kept myself away during my time at the House for the most part, but didn't like not being able to come and go as I pleased. I gave her one more hug, and then she walked me back to the gates, a promise to call me as soon as she could, and I knew I'd hold my breath every moment of that wait.

Hours later, I still had no call but did get a text from Ramses. He'd sent a few, but this was the latest.

Ramses: So you went home. Where would that be exactly?

Why he was asking I didn't know, and his other texts had

been asking me to call him. He didn't call himself, but he really wanted me to call for some reason.

Me: Home is far away from Arizona. I'm not coming back. I'm sorry about how things ended. I know you were just trying to help that night.

My phone buzzed, but not with a text. Ramses' name flashed on my screen, and I thought about answering just because I had felt bad about how I'd been so shitty to him.

Ultimately letting the phone go to voicemail, I sent another text.

Me: Please don't call. I'm not going to answer. Goodbye, Ramses, and thank you again for what you did for me.

To cement that, I blocked his number, removing his text messages. I obviously couldn't explain to him what really happened, that I'd been kidnapped and brought back to the place that had become central to my nightmares. I needed his calls and texts to stop, so I made that happen.

One less thing I had to deal with.

The wait for Birdie I passed by either staring through the window or lying down on a bed half the size of the room. Windsor House's rooms dwarfed my old bedroom, and the whole day virtually passed before I finally got not a phone call but a text message from my friend.

Birdie: I'm so sorry, December, but you staying with me isn't going to work out. I asked Shakira and Kiki too, but no dice. I'm so sorry. I thought you'd be able to stay. It just won't work. My dad's being funny, and I couldn't get him to budge. I'm so sorry!

But she'd been so sure, and I threw my phone at the bed, not knowing what else to do. I felt like a prisoner both physically and in my own head. I told Royal I had friends, resources.

So much for those.

A knock hit my door, and I'd been so pissed the fuck off I

was almost ninety percent sure whoever it was I'd punch in the goddamn face. Especially if it was Royal. I'd punch him for trapping me here, for literally being my only resource for survival. I most certainly looked amped the fuck up when I opened the door and most assuredly looked pissed, so when I whipped open that door, I wasn't surprised Jax had stepped back. Like he physically stepped back like I was going to tackle him.

I didn't see what he had, or should I say... *who* until I finally came out of my head cloud and gazed down at his burly arms. He had a puppy there, *my* puppy, and she was literally huge! Hershey climbed all over Jax's arms, face, and everything. She was amped to hell too, yipping and trying to wrestle herself free.

"Jesus, Lindquist." Jax blanched, putting more distance between us. "What's your deal? I was just going to give you the damn dog. You look like you're going to hit someone."

I kind of was, but all that was forgotten as I put out grabby hands for my cute big girl. A thought triggered she might not remember me, but as soon as Jax slid her over, all that was forgotten.

She licked my face, immediately filling me with adrenaline and dopamine and all kinds of other shit I learned about in science class I couldn't think of right now.

"Oh my gosh. Oh my gosh. Oh my gosh! Hi. Hi, honey," I crooned, squeezing her. She licked my face, giving me her little dog smile, and I laughed, rubbing her. "I missed you so much. You don't even know."

The void she left couldn't be filled, my one regret taking off so quickly, but the wound from that started to mend at the feel of her in my arms again.

Jax laughed, folding his colossal arms. "Well, it seems I did good."

Not if he stole her, stole her from a friend. I shook my

head. "You didn't take her from Rosanna, did you?" That's where she'd been staying.

Jax rolled his eyes. "No, Lindquist. Hershey goes to the vet for daycare during the day while Rosanna works. Right, little girl?" He petted her like he knew her, and when she started licking *his* face, I knew he did.

My eyes widened. "So you took her from there?" I asked, not really okay with how comfortable he was with my dog. It was like they really knew each other, played with each other. Excited, Hershey actually jumped out of my arms and to the floor, and Jax got right down there with her.

"Yes, and no," he said, getting her on her back. He rubbed her belly while she wagged a leg. He looked up at me. "Well, yes, basically. The daycare she stays at is Royal's uncle's practice. You remember he's a vet, right?"

How could I forget? I'd been inside when the entire facility burned around me. If it hadn't been for quick thinking that night, Royal... I swallowed. I guess his uncle got his practice up and running again.

"He's got a new place on Wright Street, doesn't he?" he crooned at Hershey, looking pretty freakin' funny with how big he was. A boy and his dog. He flopped her ears. "Anyway, Hershey's there all day playing with the other dogs. Rosanna doesn't even know she's gone."

"And they let you just take her?"

"For the day, yeah, and every day if you want." He frowned. "I mean, unless you don't want me to take her for you..."

I hunkered down, bringing Hershey to me.

He grinned. "That's what I thought, and how about a little thank you? I did get your dog for you."

I really didn't want to owe *any* of these boys any more favors, but they kept giving me things, things I couldn't turn down like safety, shelter, and now my dog, and though I didn't really want to accept them, I felt compelled.

I played with Hershey, Jax watching me. I really did want Hershey here. But my thoughts couldn't help but wonder at what cost.

CHAPTER
SEVENTEEN

December

Jax turned out to be yet another dutiful flunky for Royal Prinze. He not only brought Hershey and returned her to the vet each day, but also got me pretty much anything I wanted. He made sure I had food and even got my clothes cleaned when I asked. I didn't have to leave my room, but did at night and in the early mornings. That seemed to be when I heard fewer voices outside my door, and I didn't hear many. In fact, so few, I idly wondered if I'd been put in this section of their Court palace so I wouldn't be around a lot of people. I saw no one, not even the boys, outside of Jax who checked on me daily. He'd bring Hershey before school in the morning, giving me updates like how she'd been fed or if she needed to be walked, and it truly showed the power of Royal's hand. He had this guy doing whatever he wanted, all of them.

Even me.

I mean, I was in his place, on his turf and doing exactly what he wanted. Realizing that, I did start to go out more, keeping to myself as I passed staff and stayed in the more dormant areas of Windsor House. That proved easier to do as people didn't tend to go above the first couple floors and I was on the fourth. Over the captivity, I decided to start taking the walks I did do with Hershey out on the property a bit. This was nice because since it was so cold, people didn't go outside, but I found myself liking the cold. I never thought I would, despite the name my parents had given me, but I felt myself at home in it when my boots crushed ice and snow. Hershey made it even more fun to enjoy. Especially when it snowed. She liked to run and play in it, not the only dog at Windsor House. The guys had a ton here, like literally all kinds of breeds. They mostly ran around the House, but sometimes I'd catch a groundskeeper playing with a hound outside. That happened today, and after letting Hershey tire herself out with the other pup, we took our walk back to the House. We usually liked to walk through the stables because, well, *this place had fucking stables*. They were heated and everything, a nice way to put some warmth back in the two of us before going back to my prison. Hershey trotted happily all the way through, but the pair of us stopped suddenly at the sight of another up ahead.

Royal had his own puffer coat on, snowflakes coating the jacket and his blond locks. He wrestled them out of it, his cheeks flushed as he guided a horse back into a stall. The horse sprinkled with snowflakes too, the pair had clearly gone out for a morning ride, but he stopped when a man came charging into the stables.

I recognized the man as his dad.

Hershey and I stayed back, and I hunkered down, keeping the puppy by my side.

"What's this?" his dad asked him, some kind of paper in his hand. He wore a long wool coat, black gloves on his hands and a tight scarf around his neck. The scarf resembled the colors of Windsor Preparatory Academy, the school's blood obviously running deep in him. He started to hand the paper to Royal, but he didn't seem to need to. Barely looking at it, Royal kept pushing the horse into the stall.

"An acceptance letter to flight school," Royal said, locking up the stall. He looked at his dad. "But you can throw it away. I've got other things on my mind these days."

Petting Hershey, surprise at what Royal said rattled within me. I obviously didn't know a lot about Royal, but the fact he desired to go to flight school definitely surprised me. I didn't know why, though, just surprising.

His dad lowered the letter. "Why do I get the feeling those 'things' don't have anything to do with college?"

Royal started to leave but stopped, his dad's hand on his arm. His dad *braced* his arm, actually jolting Royal he had to stop so suddenly.

His dad stared him down. "You had no business even applying for this program."

"Then why does it matter?" Royal asked, sliding his arm out of his dad's grip. "You're getting what you want."

"Am I?" the man asked, shaking his head. "I checked, Royal. Dartmouth, Yale, and even Harvard haven't heard from you, and your acceptance letters came over a month ago."

Royal said nothing, but I noticed his hand, a dark glove clenching and unclenching at his side. His dad was rattling him, getting to him.

His dad got closer. "What are you trying to pull? Do you know *all* I've sacrificed for you? All I continue to sacrifice for you? If you did, you wouldn't be playing these games."

"Why don't you tell me, Dad?" Royal said, different than how I'd seen him with his dad before. Last time I came across them he looked almost fearful of him, but today, today he was standing up to him. Royal shook his head. "Tell me exactly what you've sacrificed for me."

His dad didn't need to say... because he hit him, actually hit him and not some tap. His dad *struck* him, socked him across his jaw with the force of a man to an enemy, and that blow sent Royal down clear to his knees.

"Royal!"

Everything stopped, the pair looking at me as I charged over with my dog at the lead. Royal's dad didn't even move, watching me, and Royal himself did too, his eyes wide as I got to my knees with him. The blow had charged his face a hot red, and when I attempted to touch him, he moved away.

Soft green irises ignited like emerald fire, Royal's gaze leaving me and shifting to his dad.

His dad lifted his chin. "I recognize you. Rowan Lindquist's girl, right?" He looked at Royal. "Is she staying here?"

Royal moved his jaw a little, his nod subtle as his gaze averted. How quickly he'd gone back into a shell beneath the man before him, the position of power shifting. It pissed me off, and even though Royal wouldn't let me touch him, I stayed close. I didn't know what I could do, but I wasn't leaving his side.

His dad pocketed a hand. "Change that," he said, and before I knew it he was crinkling up the paper, the acceptance letter to flight school. He tossed it at Royal. "And get rid of that. I don't want to hear anything about it again."

He started to walk away, but Royal said his name, a soft but present, "Dad…"

It was enough to make the man turn. He wet his lips. "You'll do what I say. You owe me at least that for taking your mother and sister away from me."

My eyes widened, but Royal closed his lips, looking away. His dad charged into the winter air, and when the stable closed, I reached for Royal again.

He didn't let me, standing.

"Royal—"

He whipped around. "You get off on watching shit like this? Spying on me?"

I had before, *seen* him before with his dad. I approached. "Of course not."

He shook his head, his hands up. "What are you doing out here?"

I gazed down at Hershey currently using her leash to wrap Royal and me together. She snugged us in, and even though Royal let her for a second, he pulled his legs out. He started to walk away, but I called him.

"You shouldn't let him hit you," I said, completely over-stepping here, but I didn't care. He took that, took it so easily like it'd been done before. For all I knew it could have, many, *many* times, and I saw that in his eyes when he faced me. I cringed. "And I'm sure whatever happened with your mom and sister—"

He closed the distance between us in seconds, his finger pointed at me. "Don't think you know me or know anything about me and my family. My dad may be an asshole, but that doesn't mean I don't deserve it."

Shocked he said that, I stood back.

Especially because of what he said next.

"I never should have let Knight bring you back here," he said, the words a hard swallow in his throat. He dampened full lips. "You need to go. I can arrange for—"

"I'll be out tonight," I stated, making him blanch. I nodded. "And I don't need any more favors from you."

The heat in his eyes alleviated a little, and his lips parted, like he wanted to protest.

He didn't.

He walked away, leaving me in the stables with Hershey. The door slammed shut behind him, and I fell to my knees. I stayed there for a little while.

But after that, I made a call.

CHAPTER
EIGHTEEN

Royal - Age 16

"God, you're such a ho."

So she'd noticed my hair, the lipstick on my jacket. Girls tended to like marking me these days.

Smirking, I only shook my head to find Paige Lindquist on my bed. I left my window open, always had since we were kids. We did that for each other.

"Fuck your judgment," I said, teasing, then got serious when I noticed the bag by my bed. I frowned. "You staying?"

She had before, for a little while. My dad couldn't fucking know about that shit, but it got easier and easier to hide things from him since he spent so much of his time juggling himself between Model A and Model B. I guess the apple didn't fall far from the tree.

Paige crossed her legs at the ankles, on her cell phone. She shrugged. "Dad caught me in my room with a girl."

"So who's hoing now?"

She directed a finger. "Okay, so not okay for you to say that. I'm a girl, you bitch, so take your slut-shaming somewhere else, and yes, you're a ho because every time I come over here, I got to check and see if you and one or *three* will already be in here before I come in."

"Last I checked, you took one or two of those from me before," I stated, eyeing her.

She grinned. "It's not my fault I'm hotter than you."

I made a face when she said that. Paige Lindquist hadn't been a member of the opposite sex to me since we were kids when I realized she was more of a bro than a chick. I stripped off my shirt, tossing it for another.

She looked up over her phone. "You going somewhere?"

"A party," I said, working it on, and she shook her head.

"From life number one to life number two. You think you'd be tired after schmoozing all night with the other royalty from the Court kingdom."

She always had something to say about the Court, and I didn't blame her. It took me away a lot, away from her and our friendship, but I couldn't help it with the opportunities the affiliation to the Court allowed me. I basically got free rein of any college I wanted, connections, and though I felt bad about leaving her all the time, it didn't have to be that way. She could be involved with the Court and take advantage of all the perks too. She just chose not to.

"You know you can go to these things with me," I stated, tucking just the front of my shirt in. "Join Court?" It'd never been done before, a girl joining the Court without dating or being married to one of the guys, but everybody loved Paige. If me, Jax, Knight, LJ, and the other guys fought for her, she'd get in. I frowned. "You stopped coming to these things with me, but you didn't have to."

And I never got that. We went to so many of these Court events together when she first moved here and we became friends. That first one had been something, the two of us getting into all kinds of shit and working my dad's nerves. He got on me pretty bad that night, but for the first time, I hadn't cared. I hadn't been… scared.

Paige made me different, better, and I didn't care about all the shit with my dad. It made it all a lot easier to deal with.

Paige actually lowered her cell phone after what I said, and I figured she'd say something like she always did, how the Court was a cult or some other shit like that.

"Paige?" I questioned. Paige Lindquist was never one to lack for words, but she was now.

She shrugged, passive about it. "I just don't like going."

"You just don't like going," I parroted. I tossed my dress shirt at her, and she caught it easily, one of the best on the lacrosse team with me.

She balled it up. "Things just got weird that last time we went, with one of the guys there?" She rolled her eyes. "He got handsy, and it freaked me out, I guess."

I froze, seeing nothing but red.

"What the fuck are you talking about?" I asked, coming over. "Who got handsy with you?"

We'd literally been all of *twelve* the last time the pair of us went to one of these things together, so if someone came after her, touched her…

"Oh, bro down, caveman. It's not a big deal."

"*Paige*," I gritted. "Who? Did someone touch you?"

"No, I didn't let him," she said, sitting up and looking like she accomplished something. "And I'm not telling you who because you'll go make a thing of it."

"You're damn right I'll make it a thing. If some… sick bastard was trying to touch a kid, then yeah, I'm going to make a thing of it."

She eyed me. "It wasn't like that. Anyway, I handled myself. Kicked him right in his balls."

I didn't like how she was passing this off, nor how I didn't know about it for literally four fucking years. I sat on the bed. "Why didn't you tell me?"

Her head titled. "You wouldn't have been able to do anything about it. Anyway, I'm good. So please. Stop."

She pushed me, and I grabbed her. "Paige…"

"You know what? I'm thinking I'm going to go to this party of yours," she said, doing what she did best. She averted anything from herself, always protecting, protecting me, and had *since* we were kids. She didn't know it, but she always acted like a buffer for me with my dad. Her very presence in my life frustrated the shit out of him, and he gave up on me. He stopped trying to force me to do things and washed his hands. Both the mental and sometimes physical burden of him stopped. He just stopped caring, and I had too, the need to please and try to earn my dad's forgiveness from what happened so many years ago gone. I'd given up on him too, both of us done with each other.

That could be the greatest gift this girl on my bed ever gave me, and because of that, I let this go, but only for the time being. We'd be talking about this again, but I knew how she was. I couldn't push Paige too hard or she reverted. She ran. She kept playing on her phone, and I stood, switching out my shoes.

"One second," she said, taking more than a sec. She stuck her tongue out at me when I eyed her. "Just a second."

"It's been more than a damn second." I took the phone from her. "Come on. We going?"

She took it back. "Chill the fuck down. My sister's going on some date with a guy, and I'm trying to talk her down off a cliff about what to wear. It's the first since that tool Dean."

Paige didn't talk a lot about her sister or really, hardly any personal stuff, but that thing with Dean I'd heard about. She hadn't said much about that either, but I knew the guy hurt her sister in some way.

Paige thrust her phone at me. "Tell her the pink one looks the best. I need to go to the bathroom and change my tampon."

I made a face again, another one of the joys of having a female best friend. I sat on the bed, but before doing what she told me to I clicked on the picture. Her sister, December, wore a pink dress, one that hugged her hips and made her curves superior to probably ninety percent of the girls I'd screwed in our junior class, and I'd screwed a lot of them. Paige was right. I was a complete ho and un-the-fuck-ashamed.

I scrolled to the next picture, her sister in a black dress this time and completely gorgeous. I'd never tell Paige that. It'd probably freak her out and make her hit me or something.

"*The black one's best,*" I texted to her sister, smiling at how her eyes complemented it. She had this long dark hair, thick and perfect with how it fell across her shoulders. It also worked well with the color of the dress, amazingly well. I smiled again. "*You look beautiful.*"

Honest about that, I put the phone down, and when Paige returned, she picked up her cell. After reading what I sent her sister, she threw a pillow at me. "I said to tell her the pink one."

"The black looks better." I waggled my eyebrows. "You want me to lie?"

She blew a raspberry, her gaze going to her phone. "She said thanks," Paige stated, but then her eyes flashed up. "You called her beautiful?"

Shrugging, I threw an arm around my friend's neck, wrestling with her out of the room. I got a sock in the gut for that, but I didn't care. I wasn't going to lie to her sister, no reason to.

CHAPTER
NINETEEN

December - Present

Rosanna said I could come stay with her and her family… but only if I went back to school. She also said she was going to tell my dad what's going on, which was the main reason I didn't tell her I was back in town in the first place. I knew she'd tell my dad and probably felt obligated to morally. I mean, she worked for him, so yeah, I pretty much knew she was going to tell him. Needless to say, my phone started ringing with Dad's calls again, and my aunt's weren't far behind.

"You need to talk to him," Rosanna had said that first night. She put me up in her daughter's room, her oldest away at college. Rosanna had three kids, the housekeeper a single parent, I guess.

I told her I'd agree to her demands. I'd go to school, but that didn't mean I'd be talking to my father. I was still mad at him and my aunt, so no, I wasn't talking to either of them. Frequent calls I could deal with and did, if anything to not be homeless again. It'd kinda sucked the first time, and it was cool to be able to see Rosanna again. She'd hugged me so tight when I arrived at her door, like a mom, and I didn't have too many of those in my life. I loved my aunt, but she wasn't my mom. No one could be. I only had one, and she was a pretty good one from what I remembered. She'd do exactly what Rosanna was making me do, go back to school, and while I waited for her to hammer out all those details, I got to chill with Hershey at Rosanna's. She didn't have to go to daycare with me at the house and I finally got to be with my girl legitimately. We read books and binge-watched TV while we waited for Rosanna to come home in the evenings, and one day, she didn't come back empty-handed.

About two bags full of stuff came with her, *my stuff*, and the things I left behind at my dad's. She had my school uniforms and everything, ironing them the next day for me. She also had a wool jacket for me and a matching uniform scarf.

She said they'd been my sister's.

More of my sister's hand-me-downs graced my body, my hands smoothing over a pleated skirt I paired with the coat. I could only hope this time wearing my sister's clothes didn't turn my life on its head. I didn't think I'd be able to survive a second time.

"Good luck at school today, sweetie," Rosanna said, she and her two girls at the table with bowls of cereal. She smiled small. "The school says they'll get you caught up. You should still be able to graduate."

Yippee for me.

Nodding, I genuinely thanked her for what all she'd done for me, and when I opened the door, I fully expected to take the bus.

Imagine my surprise when I saw my ride.

Hubert, my dad's driver Hubert, opened the door of a sedan for me. He took off his hat. "Happy to have you back, Ms. December. I'm here to take you to school."

Dad's orders. Though he didn't say. If my dad couldn't control me directly, he'd do so through kind-faced drivers and housekeepers.

"Good to see you too, Hubert," I said, very happy to see him as well. I got inside, getting good at holding my skirt so it didn't ride up against the seats. We took off, and my destiny awaiting, I let it happen.

I didn't have a choice.

"Ah! You're back. You're back. You're back!" came about twenty minutes later—Birdie when she, Kiki, Shakira, and about half the female basketball team waited outside my locker. They had donuts and everything, vegan donuts.

I could have cried.

I couldn't help smiling as I gave hugs to friends, true friends who were obviously looking out for me. I admit I had been a little sore about not being able to stay with Birdie, but she said it'd been her dad and that wasn't her fault. She was also by no means obligated to help me. It was what it was, and I was happy to see her now.

"Good to be back," I said, kind of sorta not lying. I was happy to see them so... I shrugged. "What did I miss?"

I immediately realized it wasn't me as we walked to first period—people taking a second to notice I was back but after that gratefully going back to their conversations. It seemed me, my situation, and my *leaked news* about my past seemed to be old hat, and Birdie put her arm around me, confirming that.

"I told you they'd all move on," she said, whispering the words while the other girls told about their college plans. Apparently, many had gotten their entrance letters while I'd been away. Many like Royal.

I tried not to think about him because anytime I did, I saw his dad. I saw him *hurting him*, and I saw Royal lashing out at me because of that. I knew that's what that was. He was probably embarrassed about what I walked in on and raged at me.

It didn't give him any excuse to treat me the way he had, but being on the outside now, I got it.

Trying to be present, I blended back into the conversations around me, all of us stopping when the headmaster, Principal Hastings, passed us.

He pulled his glasses off, noticing me. "Ms. Lindquist. Good to have you back."

I smiled. "Thanks, sir. Got a lot of work to do, though, if I want to graduate."

He nodded. "I'm sure you'll manage, and happy to see you hanging out with the right people to help you do so."

Birdie and the others smiled at him saying that, but I didn't. Before everything with Paige, the principal had given me a warning about who I hung out with. He hadn't liked seeing me with Royal and Knight for whatever reason.

My smile tight that time, I let that go, and he advised me to see the guidance counselor sometime this week. He said, "It might help," but I had a feeling that wouldn't be happening, me being helped that was. All this was still too raw, too soon.

It was all too what I was seeing when I turned around.

They came down the hallway in a pack, the Court, but at the center was the main attraction. LJ, Jax, and Knight all had girls under their arms...

But it was Royal's who wore a necklace.

The necklace beamed beneath bright red locks—Mira—when she flicked her hair over her shoulder. It was Royal who had his arm around her, hugging her close, and at seeing me, the whole party stopped. *He* stopped for a moment.

But then, he looked away.

He rushed the group on, clearly not expecting me to be here today. LJ, Jax, and Knight headed away with him, but I noticed Jax did look apologetic. In fact, *all* the guys passed a glance my way. Even Knight, his frown hard before his gaze averted too. One person who stared me *right* in the face was

Mira, her fingers twirling her necklace before pressing herself closer under Royal's arm. I couldn't see it close, but the necklace looked just like the others the girls with Court boys had, the ones in serious relationships with Court boys.

"Oh, yeah, that's new too," Birdie said, frowning. She frowned at me. She and the entire school knew Royal and I hooked up thanks to Mira. I never let on about it being more, but she had to know something was up since I'd told her he made the call to bring me to Windsor House. She touched my arm. "Yeah, that."

That, the couple walking down the hall and to what was probably their first classes. Royal and Mira together.

Mira was Court-kept.

CHAPTER
TWENTY

December

The what-the-fuckery only continued into the rest of the week. I was so far behind in school it was embarrassing, and even *before* I left, I hadn't been great at everything. I was sent home daily with a stack of books, and even though my friends attempted to help me, things felt beyond help. I didn't want to be here. I didn't want to be in this school and with constant reminders of what happened with my sister. Royal bopping around with Mira only drove the dagger deeper. The two were inseparable, quite literally hanging all over each other, and I just about reached my breaking point not even a full week back.

Christ.

The Bentley was parked outside of Rosanna's duplex, Hubert stopping right next to it. I honestly wondered how I managed to not see my dad sooner. He obviously knew I was home, sent Hubert for me for school and everything. Maybe he was just letting me get comfortable.

I almost told Hubert to take a drive around the block a

few hundred times, but something told me he was in on this too. He answered to my dad after all. Braving up, I grabbed my bag and took the iced steps up to Rosanna's door. She gave me a key, and I opened it, expecting to see a man in a full suit from his day at work...

Not a damn intervention.

My dad was there. This was true, but there was also someone else, and that someone shot to her feet the moment she saw me.

My aunt Celeste, *Aunt C.* was here and all the way from California. She threw her arms around me, holding me close. "Oh, December, I could strangle you."

I held her back, my heart severing in two. I missed her. I did, but...

I opened my eyes, peering over her shoulder to my dad. He sat on Rosanna's couch, Hershey on the sofa next to him. She had her little head on his lap, sleeping.

I guess dogs on the couch were okay when it wasn't his own.

He stared at me, a hand on Hershey's head. The two had gotten a little closer before I left, but I figured he'd just been putting up with her. He stood, my puppy waking up but only to go to the kitchen. Rosanna handed him tea, tea she'd been making. She was a servant in her own house to her employer.

I closed my eyes, holding my aunt again. Why they were both even here besides being out of obligation for their daughter and niece was beyond me. And maybe that was all this was, obligation.

"I didn't mean to scare you," I said to my aunt, meaning that. She'd taken care of me most of my life.

She pulled back, my heart aching how much the middle-aged woman looked like my mother. She always did, the soft features and everything. She touched my face. "You didn't scare me. You broke my heart. We already lost your sister, and you pull this? Running away?"

I called her on that about Paige. She'd dismissed my sister

just as much as Dad had, telling me not to get my hopes up about the lost cause who constantly ran away.

I let go of her, easing back, and the two watched me like I'd run again. I idly wondered if this *was* some kind of intervention, a damn bust and officers would come pouring into the room to take me away and force me to do what they said. They couldn't do that to me. Not legally, and that was the only thing keeping me in this room and not running for the hills.

"Please sit down, December." The first words my dad spoke to me. He put a hand toward the sofa, and I did take it, my puppy bounding over to me.

I scrubbed her behind the ears. "Is this an intervention?" I actually asked them, but no one laughed but me. Rosanna shook her head from the kitchen, gazing away, and my dad's look could murder.

His frown narrowed his eyes. "I suppose you think this is all funny? Your sister died, you skip town, and this is all just completely hilarious to you? Humorous?"

He almost broke me with that, made those tears fall again, but I refused. I swallowed. "Nothing's funny about wanting space. I thought you two would be happy."

"Happy?" they said together, and I swear to God that'd been the first time they were on the same position about anything.

I nodded. "I heard you guys talking. In Aunt C.'s room?" That conversation still chilled me, all the pain that day coming back in a wash, and I shook my head. "I was releasing the burden of me off the both of you."

The two exchanged a look with each other, and it'd been Aunt C. to close her eyes, come to me. My dad, on the other hand, stood his ground, looking away when he pushed hands into his pockets.

I had no idea what was worse in the next moments, my aunt suddenly groveling before me that what I heard wasn't true or my dad being completely dismissive. They both came across as just ridiculous, and I wanted to end whatever this was.

My aunt touched my face. "It's not true, December. I've always wanted you in my life."

Well, she had a shitty way of showing it. I blinked away, and my aunt shot a look at my dad.

"Tell her what she heard was a mistake, Rowan," she commanded, nostrils flaring. "Tell her you don't feel that way. Fight for her."

She called him out, called him right there, and my dad put down his tea, coming over to me.

"Do you want to stay here?" he asked, surprising me. His jaw moved. "Because if you do, I... well, I think it's best."

"Rowan!"

"I think it's safe for you and," he continued, his eyes averting, "I think you should stay."

My lips closed, surprised at this but not really. I was getting what I wanted, wasn't I? I didn't want to go back to my dad's and under his rules and regulations...

So why did I feel socked in the gut?

I picked up Hershey, leaving my aunt's hands as I left the room and rounded a corner.

"What is wrong with you?" I heard my aunt cry, physically crying, and I did too, tears pushing through my lids. I touched my head against the wall, only to jump upon hearing a door slam. I assumed it was my aunt, and I was right when I turned my head. She'd left, only my dad and Rosanna in the room.

"Make sure you watch her," he said to her. "That she's safe, and Hubert will be looking out for her too. And let me know... well, anything. Just anything, and if she needs anything... yes, you know."

How he pretended to care even now, still pretending.

I closed my eyes again.

CHAPTER
TWENTY-ONE

December

We cruised slowly toward holiday break, twinkling lights lining the streets and restaurants in Maywood Heights. People were preparing for the season, gearing up, and meanwhile, I was attempting not to have a nervous breakdown. I started getting anxiety after that meeting with my aunt and dad, it all getting worse, and I felt more and more buried under homework and stress. While others were getting psyched for their holiday parties and final exams, I was freaking out. I had a feeling graduation in the spring wouldn't be an option for me, and it wasn't like I cared much, but it was literally all I had. Lunches were filled with banter about what schools people were going to next year, and I just got to sit with my vegan chili, watching it all happen around me like I wasn't a part of my body. I watched life continue on while I became more and more dead inside, and I hated it. I hated everything. I was even starting to feel a certain way about Rosanna. I knew she was looking out for me, but after that confrontation at the house, I felt like I was being watched. Like if I stepped out of line or did something off, she'd immediately report said thing to my father. It was making me hella paranoid, and that lingered amongst what used to be a pretty easygoing relationship. Nothing visibly changed between us, but I felt it inside. I was starting to feel not welcome in her house because of the feeling. Especially since holiday break was coming up and her daughter would be returning from school. I figured once that happened, I'd be reverting to the couch or something, a nuisance in her house, and I hated that feeling.

"Did you ask your dad about... well, you know?" I asked Birdie at the beginning of second period one day. We'd taken our seats in Mr. Pool's class.

I knew her answer before she even said anything.

She played with her pen, leaning in. "I'm sorry. I asked about you staying over break, but Dad's still being weird. Maybe it's because we'll have a lot of family coming through? Anyway, you can always stay the night, though. Anytime you want. You know that."

I had a couple of times, and her dad was really cool, which was why I was surprised he kept saying no about an extended stay. I mean, it was his house and stuff, but he literally bent over backwards when any of the girls or I came over to Birdie's house. He was the epitome of a single dad trying to take care of his baby girl, made us food and always asked us if we needed anything.

Figuring I couldn't come for the reason she said, I decided to not take offense. I nodded, sliding back into my chair. Getting my books out, I attempted not to take notice when a certain cool scent flooded into the room like a fragrance commercial. Royal was followed by his bro family, Jax, LJ, and Knight, all four with the same English class as me.

The boys placed their bags down, bantering with each other, and they did that until the start of class. They didn't acknowledge me too much anymore, any glances or other forms of acknowledgment fading quickly the day I'd seen them all in the hallway with Mira. I supposed it had started slow with them ghosting me, progressive, but eventually, we arrived to the place we were now. I was in the same universe as them, but outside of physically running into them, none of us even looked at each other. Let alone carried on conversation. As far as I was concerned, that was just grand. If Royal had so quickly moved on to Mira when things had been "too hot" with me, then whatever about it. He was obviously a jerk, and I picked up on that pretty early in our relationship, but had written it off. He fooled me, and he'd done it well.

Royal and crew in my periphery, I let that all go, and focused on more important things. I wasn't about to be held back in school because of the likes of Royal Prinze and his following. I was going to graduate with the rest of our senior class, then move on to bigger and better things. Class started at the top of the hour, and Mr. Pool immediately went into talks about the neoclassical period. I actually knew this, so I stayed present during the hour, and as class started winding down, Mr. Pool paused us. He got a knock at the door, and when he called over, the door opened. A boy wearing a Windsor Preparatory uniform came in, a boy with messy brown curls and extremely extended height. He had to dip his head a little just to come inside.

No way…

"We have a new arrival today, class," Mr. Pool said, his hands on the boy's shoulders, his hands on *Ramses'* shoulders. The boy grinned, facing the class like an audience, and I rose up in my chair, a huge "What the fuck?" on my lips. But that was Ramses clear as day, *my* Ramses. Well, not mine, but the boy I worked with in Arizona. Mr. Pool shook his shoulders. "Some of you may recognize Mr. Mallick from your freshman year. Well, he's back. Recently transferred from…"

"Crestfire Hills Prep, Mr. Pool," he stated, those same dark eyes that eyed me many times. They currently resided on Mr. Pool, the man introducing him.

"Crestfire Hills Prep," Mr. Pool continued, seriously grinning his ass off. "He was one of my star pupils freshman year, and we're happy to have him back. Ramses will be finishing his senior year with us, class, and I'm sure Crestfire Hills will be kicking themselves to have let you go. I'm sure you'll be leading the class soon, just as you had four years ago."

Ramses' long fingers went to the back of his neck. Clearly, all of this a little too much for him, but he was here and with people bragging on him about his smarts as he did himself.

My back hit the chair, all of this wild. The odds we'd come from the same town freaked me the fuck out, and now, he was suddenly back *at the end* of the term. Ramses' gaze soon flittered over the crowd, Mr. Pool advising him to take any seat he wanted. I believed his eye may stop on me, recognize me, but he never made it that far, his attention stopping toward the back of the class.

I turned and easily found out why. Royal, LJ, Knight, Jax, and the rest of their Court bros usually goofed off through most of class, but needless to stay, they weren't now. They stared ahead, very much aware of this new arrival, and when I faced away, a tall boy with extended height passed me. Ramses flew right by me with his long strides, taking the vacant seat behind me and facing forward, and I wondered if he noticed me in his class. I mean, he hadn't said anything, and I hadn't seen if he saw me or not.

A tap touched my back, and I shifted only to have a note fall to my front.

I caught it, making sure Mr. Pool's back was turned before I opened it.

What's up, Arizona?

I nearly laughed at it. I guess he'd seen me. I started to turn, but Mr. Pool spoke, mentioning something about tonight's homework assignment.

"Until tomorrow, friends," Mr. Pool ended up concluding with. The bell ringing, he smiled. "We'll get you geared up for those final exams yet."

The groan through class radiated as students packed up. Ramses stood and passed me again before I could say anything. At the door, he pointed a finger outside it, grinning at me before going out, and I shook my head once more. I followed the flood out into the hallways, and the moment I spotted the tall-as-hell boy, I punched him in the uniform jacket.

"What the hell, *Arizona*?" I said, mocking him and what he said. That place was more his than mine. I shoved him a little. "What are you even doing here?"

"Trying to avoid assault. Jesus," he stated, chuckling. He cradled his arm. "My first day, and I'm already getting my ass kicked."

"Oh, whatever. That didn't even hurt."

"Totally did."

I shoved him again, and he nearly ran into Birdie, the girl somehow dwarfed by this guy in size when she was already a head and a half taller than me. At the sight of Ramses, she lost her shit, though. He did too, and when the duo proceeded to do a fist bump handshake, I did a double take.

"Birdie Arnold," he said, coming out of the shake with a snap. "Long time."

"Really fucking long time." She grinned, then nudged him herself. "What are you doing here, kid?"

"Just living life. Figured I'd transfer back since y'all *clearly* missed me. I mean, were you guys actually doing anything in class before I got here? Mr. Pool looked damn desperate in there."

She got him in the arm again and he took *her* under his arm, the two coming up long enough to finally see me and my wide eyes. Ramses smiled. "December, Birdie and I used to hang in the same circles."

"Wait. *You guys* know each other?" Birdie moved a finger between us.

I rolled my eyes. "Long story. Ramses got me a job when I was in AZ."

"Sure did," he stated, dropping an arm around Birdie's shoulders. "And December promptly ran for the hills not long after. The referral sure did turn out well for me."

"I'm sure to get away from your ass." She mock-socked him in the stomach, making him laugh. She pushed him by the chest. "And way to downplay how we know each other." She directed a finger right at him. "This kid was a legend when he went to school here. Seriously, an all-star."

I twitched. "An all-star at what?"

Ramses lifted his head of dark curls. "I used to play basketball."

"*Used* to play?" Birdie asked, hands on her hips. "What the hell happened? You burned up the court when you were here."

My lips parted. Ramses a jock? I never would have thought that with the exception of our final hours together. His friends had looked like jocks, and he fit right in with them. Then there was his height and everything, so I guess that made sense.

Ramses shook his head. "Decided to focus on my brain. Dad's cut me off, remember? Have to pay for college myself."

"Ah, that's right." Birdie frowned. "Resident bad boy got himself shipped off to desert country. How was that over there with the tumbleweeds BTW?"

"Way better than here." Ramses frowned now, but didn't let it linger. The warning bell for our next class started, and Birdie came out from under his arm.

She bumped his fist. "Talk to me about it all at lunch. And the other girls too. You always got a seat at our table."

He tipped a chin at her, giving her one last bump before she started down the opposite end of the hallway. My class, on the other hand, went the other way, and after saying goodbye to Birdie too, I started to tell Ramses I needed some answers as well. Like why Birdie had called him a "bad boy" when he'd been king of the uber nerds when I knew him. Also him getting cut off? What the hell? And why was he here? The questions traveled my brain in influx, but all that ceased when the pair of us suddenly weren't alone.

Royal and crew came outside Mr. Pool's class. They'd stayed in there for some reason, way last to leave, and upon surfacing from the room, they found Ramses and me. Green eyes, Royal's, connected with me for only moments before passing to Ramses.

"Prinze," Ramses said to him, his hands sliding into his uniform pockets. Royal, on the other hand, didn't acknowledge him at all. He merely looked at me, frowning before going the opposite way with the other boys. Jax, Knight, and LJ gave Ramses a little *eyeing* themselves, and I remembered what Ramses told me about what sent him running from this place. He said he had a run-in with a clique.

That apparent clique ventured down the hallway, bags on their arms and big backs, and shaking his head, Ramses looked at me.

"What are your plans next hour?" he asked me, cutting off my sight from Royal when he stood in front of me. "Feel like taking a walk?"

CHAPTER
TWENTY-TWO

Royal - Age 17

A locker slammed in my face, and since I knew why, I looked the other way. I decided to lace up my lacrosse cleats instead, busying myself with the task.

That only pissed Paige off more.

"What the *hell* did you think you were doing?" she gritted, getting in *my* face when I was the last person she should have been mad at. She propped hands on her hips. "Royal?"

Some of our teammates bumped a fist on my shoulder, passing us both with grins on their face and lacrosse sticks in their hands. We had practice today, a practice to get ready for.

"Why aren't you dressed?" I asked, noticing my teammate was still in her street clothes. She was allowed in the guys' locker room, the only girl ever in recorded history. She'd broken a lot of barriers, my best friend, and I'd been there along the way to help her do it. I continued to do that, be there for her.

She shook her head. "You were so out of line."

"Actually, I think I was completely in line," I told her. My cleats laced, I grabbed my lacrosse stick off the bench. "I got a monster off the streets and off our field."

Coach Marshall had been nothing but a sick bastard, the epitome of the scum of the earth, and she was in my face talking about him.

"What if people find out," she started, but stopped when more guys came through. LJ and Jax stopped, Knight behind them.

"Everything okay?" LJ asked, ready for this confrontation with me. I recruited all the guys in the end to help, power in numbers. I needed the truth, needed *facts* to help support what I needed to do. LJ, Jax, and Knight helped me find those facts, and even though they hadn't been affected, we had friends who were. We had *Paige*, the most important thing. Someone hurting her was a slam against all of us as far as the group and I were concerned. We were family, there for each other.

Paige's eyes widened at the acknowledgment. I was sure she didn't love more of her business being out there, but I personally didn't care.

"Everything's cool," I told them, letting them go, and Paige covered her arms.

"What's happened to you?" she asked. "Getting them in on this? Getting in my business—"

"He touched you," I said, a finger in her face. I snorted. "He put hands on you, and I stopped that, stopped him from doing that to anyone else." It took me a while, well over a year, but I figured out exactly *who* in our Court family had come after her as a kid…

And why hadn't I seen it sooner? More than one guy on the team had reported looks, *stares* from our former head coach while they'd been in the shower or doing whatever. It only took a few guys, only a few coming forward when asked around, and I put together the pieces. The guy was a sick fuck, and I finally found him. He'd been one of our few alumni that showed up to everything, always talking to all the kids and even cornered me a time or two.

I'd been lucky when other guys hadn't. I'd been lucky when *she* hadn't. I swallowed. "That guy's going to rot in a jail cell for what he did to you."

"For what he did to me?" She had tears in her eyes, and I didn't know what pissed me off more, the fact she was obsessed that I blew the whistle on a child predator or the fact she didn't care enough about herself to do the same. Her jaw worked. "We don't have a coach because of you, but everyone will *think* its because of me. Everyone will know about a stupid thing that happened so fucking long ago it doesn't matter."

"It does matter," I challenged. "It matters because of you. Paige... I was just fucking looking out for you."

"Well, no one asked you to do that," she said, tears in her eyes. "I swear to God, Royal Prinze. You and your toxic masculinity. You think you can do anything since you got that silver ring on your finger. Even mess around in my life."

I gripped it. "Not true."

"Oh, isn't it? And what's really fucked up is you don't even care about all that. In fact, you hate it. You loathe it but deal with it because of your dad, a guy who's beaten the shit out of you since we were kids, and for some reason you still feel the need to impress him?" She shook her head. "News flash, Royal. What happened to your mom and sister was an accident and had nothing to do with a *six*-year-old boy—"

"Watch it," I gritted. "Stop right now."

"Or what?" she challenged, getting in my face now. "Because you'll hurt me? Raise your hand and throw down the gauntlet on me like you did Coach?"

I couldn't hear, the ringing in my ears too loud. She'd

never said such things to me... *cut* me in such a way and I couldn't see straight. She'd never do that to me, not her.

I think she saw that, witnessed the complete shutdown currently raging a war inside me. She cried then, actual tears cutting down her cheeks, and when she walked away, I grabbed her.

"Paige..."

She collapsed, falling literally into my arms, and I gripped her, not letting her fall.

"Paige?" I asked, freaked the fuck out. She said things she'd never say, crying like this... I shook my head. "Paige, what's going on?"

She gripped me back, quivering and wailing, and I knew something else was going on here, something deep that would make her act this way. This wasn't just about what we were talking about, couldn't be.

"She's married," whispered so softly in my ear I barely even heard it. She buried her face into my neck. "She's married, Royal, and I'm... I've been so stupid."

It took me a minute to register what she was saying, so many words said.

I closed my eyes. She had been seeing someone, acting so different from herself but in such a good way. I'd seen my friend... happy, legitimately happy, and possibly for the first time. She and I had a lot of pain from both our fathers, a lot a pain, but we always pulled through. We always rose above.

I dampened my lips. "Who?" I asked. "Tell me who, Paige."

Her mouth closed, her headshake adamant against my neck, and I knew she wouldn't tell me. At least not now.

"What do you need?" I said instead, all of this taking everything within me not to run out of here like an ape and fix whatever this was. To make someone *hurt* for hurting my best friend. Maybe Paige was right. Maybe I had turned into something bad. Maybe there was more than one kind of monster.

"Just this, Royal," she said, making me come down from it all. She squeezed me harder. "Just this."

I gave her that, knowing exactly what I'd do if she changed her mind. I'd be ready. I'd fix this for her.

I'd do whatever she wanted me to do.

CHAPTER
TWENTY-THREE

December - Present

The last thing I needed to be doing this close to finals was skipping class, but I had way too many questions at the moment to not delve into things deeper with Ramses. His quote, unquote "walk" ended up leading us out into the snow and to a part of campus I'd never been before. The greenhouse was heated, gorgeous with winter blooms, and I studied some of them, taking off my coat and sitting near the koi pond. The school had some of those, their wispy tails fluttering through the water.

"I see you still know your way around this place," I said, putting my coat on a rock formation next to the pond. They had them everywhere.

Ramses opted out of a coat for our journey, his uniform jacket apparently enough. It seemed he was paying for that because he didn't take his jacket off like I did upon entering the greenhouse. He warmed his long arms, and my mind was blown that he was even here and we were together right now.

"Not a lot of things change, I guess," he started, smiling at the pond, then found me. "Well, I guess a lot of things. You're here now."

"And why does it feel like you're not surprised by that?" I asked, eyeing him. "Me being here?"

"Maybe because I'm not." He made a turn, tugging a bloom under a heat lamp. Dark eyes shifted my way. "I followed you that night."

"Followed me?"

He nodded. "After you made me drop you off in that completely sketch neighborhood, I doubled back. I lost you, of course. You weren't where I left you but after going around the neighborhood for a bit I saw you. I saw you and friggin' *Knight Reed*."

My lips closed, unaware he'd been there, nor how much he'd seen. I still got chills from that night and what might have happened had Knight not been there.

"I mean, he was wailing on a motherfucker," he said, letting me know he did see something. "And after, you got in a car with him."

"He saved me," I explained, not happy with the way he went about that, then dragged me back home, but at least he'd gotten there in time. I shrugged. "That guy was the shop owner I stole from that first day we met, and yeah, I did steal from him. The only time I was... I was, well, hungry."

Ramses' eyes surprisingly softened at that. He folded long arms. "Well, that explains a lot, but not really why Knight Reed was there in the first place. I mean, I was like what the fuck? But then I remembered the off-the-wall things about you."

I smirked. "Off-the-wall things?"

He gripped his curls. "Well, how about the fact you were looking at articles that happened in my hometown? I mean, that news story went viral in the surrounding areas but not really to the point of nationally. Also, that conversation you were having in the bathroom. The fact you were homeless..."

"You going to make a point here anytime soon, Mallick?" I asked, using what was apparently his last name.

He grinned. "Sure am, Arizona." He stood, venturing over. He opened his hands. "Got me thinking I should look back at those articles you were looking at, and when I did, things started to make more sense. They never said Paige had a sister, but you obviously had her last name. I put two and two together after that, that there was a relation there. You obviously came from that town, *ran* from that town after what happened."

I closed my lips. "And so you're here now to…"

"I honestly don't know," he said with a chuckle. "I called you hoping to hammer some of this out, but you ghosted me."

"Can you blame me? All that with Knight was completely fucked up."

He frowned. "Why was he there even?" But then he stopped, closing his lips. "He's your sister's friend, good friend? And if I know that barbarian, he probably thought he was looking out for you."

My eyes widened at how he'd gotten that so spot on. I nodded. "Yeah, that's why he came. Royal sent him actually."

"Dude's still fucking crazy, I see," he stated, shaking his head. "His rise to the throne has obviously expedited since I originally left, but he was still crazy-obsessed with the Court. He and his friends do anything they want."

"So what's the deal with you guys anyway," I asked, standing. "And why *are* you here? Not because of me?" Because that would be a little much. I mean, we'd been coworkers, yeah, and had maybe started to become friends, but we weren't that close.

He dampened his lips. "I used to be into the Court stuff too. Remember that clique I mentioned?"

I nodded. "You said you had a run-in with them."

"That's true, and when I didn't like being 'a part of the

party' anymore," he air-quoted, "Royal and his pack of Court minions didn't just throw me shade, they made my life hell. It was hell, and they let me know that. It's hard to explain. You just know it when you see it. They turned the school on me."

"You know it when you see it…"

He was right about that, and I chewed the inside of my cheek.

"And I guess maybe part of the reason I'm here is because of you," he continued, surprising me. He shrugged. "The way I saw you leave was fucked, and yeah, I wanted to make sure you were okay, but I also didn't like what I saw with Knight. It showed me those guys are still doing shit, and with me being so far ahead in school, I basically said fuck it. I wanted to come back. Let them see me, and what do I care now? We're about to graduate."

Why did he care now? I saw what he was saying, but they were almost done, *we* were almost all done with school, so what did it all matter about them "seeing him"? I could only chock that up to something deeper going on inside him, something that wasn't my business and he had to work out on his own.

I shook my head at him. "Another person coming to 'look out for me'?" I rolled my eyes. "You know that's why Royal sent Knight, right?"

He nodded, obvious since I said as much. "And is there anything wrong with someone looking out for you? I wished I had that way back when. My dad's so obsessed with the Court he took their side, allowed them to bully me, and I gave him so much shit about it he shipped me off to basically shut me up."

"And cut you off?" I asked, remembering what was said between him and Birdie.

He frowned. "Yeah, but he's offered a peace offering with me coming back. I'm on my best behavior, I might get my money."

I shoved him. "So much for looking out for me."

He lifted big palms, chuckling. "What? You thought it was all about you?"

I hit him again, but was happy it wasn't. I liked Ramses, but if he was willing to uproot schools for me, he might feel he had a connection with me a little deeper than I was comfortable with. He was good-looking enough and a nice person, but I wasn't interested in him in that way. Especially not now. Boys were way too much drama for me, and I had a track record.

I crossed my arms. "Well, I'm happy you're here. I've had my own run-in with the Court, so it's nice to have friends."

That didn't settle well on his face, but when the bell alarmed across the campus, signaling the end of *third* period, he kept whatever opinions he had about that to himself. He faced the school, and I did too.

"Probably should go back before I bury myself even deeper with how far behind I am," I said, getting my coat on. "That month being away messed me up. I might not even graduate. Especially if I fail my finals."

I expected some kind of sympathetic response from Ramses with what I said. Not a damn grin, but that's what he gave me. He flicked out his jacket lapels. "Well, I guess it's good you have Dr. Brain here at your service. I can tutor you. No problem."

No, this guy did *not* just call himself Dr. Brain. I chuckled. "I'll take all the help I can get."

CHAPTER
TWENTY-FOUR

December

Ramses failed to mention something during his first week at Windsor Prep. Ramses was... popular, and not just any kind of popular, uberly so to the point where being in his wake kind of got me pushed out during some conversations. He hung with Birdie, Shakira, Kiki, and me at the beginning of the week, but by the end, basically, we were hanging with him. Whatever damage the Court had done to his rep prior to him leaving had obviously dissipated, and pretty much *everyone* knew him. Even kids who couldn't have possibly gone to school while he'd been here, Ramses pulling both guys and girls in for hugs in the hallway. He'd clearly built something before he got here and was quickly getting right back into it. It was wild, like Court-status popularity but different. Where people usually cowered in fear upon seeing someone from the Court, they did the opposite with Ramses Mallick. They acknowledged and laughed with Ramses, pointing toward him with props when he passed by. He'd done so back every time, knowing *everybody's* name, and I mean everybody. He may have been gone for the last three years, but he obviously hadn't forgotten anybody. At lunch, he pretty much built a rapport, and his table was basically the hot new lunch spot to eat at. Birdie said she'd save him a spot to eat with us, but we ended up eating with him, him and the rest of the boys' basketball and wrestling teams. I guess that was the clique he hung out with back in the day. Oh, them and the IT nerds. He literally had friends everywhere, people just short of selling tickets to eat lunch with him and see where he'd been. He told that story too, and I felt like I heard it a hundred times. He'd become a world traveler apparently, going away to boarding school and to the rough deserts of Arizona. The whole thing I found humorous, genuinely having me laugh, since what I knew about him was pretty laid-back. It was a switch from how things used to be, humor and I decided I'd take laughs where I could get them. They were welcomed definitely. Things had been way easier this past week, and I didn't find myself looking at the Court and what they were doing all the time. I still noticed them, of course, how couldn't I?

That happened when people gave you the stink eye.

That stink eye hadn't been for me per se, but clearly for Ramses, the new/old kid who suddenly had their table a little less occupied these days. I mean, they still had a crap-ton of people over there. Like all the time, but the weight it lost I definitely noticed. We over here had gained it.

Eating my tofu today, I glanced up from time to time, seriously trying not to still be pissed the fuck off that Mira and Royal were together. She sat with him, of course, and though they were never all over each other, they were *together*—clearly. He kept a hand on her hip, talking while she twirled that damn necklace around her neck, and I didn't get it. I didn't get *them*. He thought we moved too fast together, okay, but that?

Shaking my head, I attempted to eat my lunch, but when I

got a nudge, I peered up. Apparently, away from his party on the other side of the table, Ramses stood above me, grinning as we waved for me to make room.

Laughing, I let him, the boy threading one long leg, then the other into a cafeteria lunch table made for normal-sized people. I swear to God, I had no idea how the tables held the capacity for the superhumans I ate with at lunch.

Getting himself nice and comfy, Ramses snatched a bite of my fried tofu, something he tended to do ever since he found out I was vegan. I swear he loved my food more than Birdie's, but that didn't stop him from getting hers too next to me. He swiped one of her chicken nuggets, getting a hard punch in the arm, and between me and her, he got his daily quota of punches for the day. He should try not stealing people's food.

I stuck my tongue out at him, making him chuckle. When he went for my apples, this time I held up my fists.

"Okay, okay," he said, raising his hands. "I'm done."

"Good." I shook my head, attempting to listen to Kiki and Shakira's conversation about their upcoming math final. They sounded pretty prepared for it, but I was still dreading mine. Ramses had started to work with me during our study period in the library, but there was only so much one could do for a lost cause. I was really behind, but he wouldn't give up. We'd been working pretty well together, and I had appreciated him taking the time when he didn't have to. I noticed him listening to the conversation too for a while, but eventually, he panned over to the Court table. He absent-mindedly chewed a fry he'd gotten from behind Birdie's back.

"So Prinze and your sister," he said, making me come out of the conversation too. He nodded over there. "They were still like joined at the hip? I know what you said before, but they were still ride-or-dies? I mean, as kids they were insepa-rable, but I know things like that can shift or change in high school a little. They were still like really, really cool?"

I brushed my hands off. "Um, yeah, as far as I know. Why?"

He shrugged big shoulders, absentmindedly chomping on Birdie's fries. In fact, he took so many that she hit him again, and he laughed.

"I'm going to kill you," she threatened.

"Oh, I'll buy you some more," he said, taking one last one before hopping out of the booth. I noticed he didn't answer my question, but in the next moment, he was throwing his long reach around Birdie and me. He faced the table. "So what does everyone think about coming to my house tonight? A small gathering, nothing big, but you're all welcome."

The table stopped, like literally everyone stopped eating.

Shakira, sitting on my other side, grinned. "Um, how about fuck yeah? Of course we're coming over."

"Sweet!" Kiki chanted, clapping and everything. "You still have the ping-pong table? Game room and movie theater?"

Movie theater? What the fuck?

Ramses grinned now. "Uh, yeah. So everybody's in, then? Like I said, it doesn't have to be anything huge. I know it's a school night and not long before finals."

The fact it was a school night and before final exams didn't phase anyone, Birdie dancing in her seat next to me. She nudged me. "Dude, you should totally get excited. Ramses' house is frickin' awesome."

Ramses rolled his eyes. "Correction. *Dad's* house. None of that stuff's mine. He and my mom just let me use it."

"Well, we will happily use it too," Shakira said, the black girl twirling one of her long braids. She eyed me. "Bro even has a basketball court."

My eyes widened. "Seriously?" I knew Ramses' family had money, but what the hell? "Who's his dad?"

"Who's his dad?" Shakira's eyes bugged out now. "Um, ever heard of Mayor Mallick? Like the mayor of Maywood Heights?"

Seriously, the *what the fuck* had to be all over my face now. I stared up at Ramses. "Uh, so never mentioned that one, Mallick."

"Never came up, 'Zona," he stated, waggling thick eyebrows at me. He'd taken to shortening my nickname recently, chuckling. "Anyway, father figure and Mom are out of town tonight, which means it's the perfect time for my friends and me to get to reap the spoils."

This had the table soaring in delight, and as I listened to the details, I did think about his dad. The mayor? Wow.

Did anyone in this town not have power?

CHAPTER
TWENTY-FIVE

December

Ramses Mallick was seriously an asshole, and I knew that the moment I woke up the next day with a serious hangover and an aversion to light. I'd pretty much drunk my weight in alcohol last night, and the weed I smoked probably reached new heights. I'd been baked to hell, and despite paying for that this morning, it'd been awesome. I couldn't remember the last time I drank and smoked not because I was stressed or even depressed. I let loose because I was having a good time with friends, a nice switch from before. Still, I was paying for that now, and it was only because of my dog I got up at all in the morning. Hershey wanted her at-the-butt-crack-of-dawn morning walk, and I tried to do that for her usually before school each day.

"God, you hate me, don't you?" I asked her, my big puppy stomping my face with her paws to get my ass up. I groaned. "Fine. Fine. *Fine*. I'm up."

Like she understood, she hopped from my bed and disappeared somewhere into the room. I was still trying to trigger a little life into my body, the visions of beer pong and video games still in my head. Ramses' house did have a game room, and we'd all spent most of the time in it, eating junk food and getting piss-ass drunk. It'd seriously been a good time, and I smiled a little, gripping my bed. My puppy came back with her leash in her mouth, wagging her tail, and that smile I had left.

"You really do hate me."

She just blasted me with that dog smile in response, and after I rubbed her head, I got up. She gave me the time to wash up and be really lazy when I put my coat on over my T-shirt and leggings. I'd dress properly when we got back, and after sticking my feet into my UGG boots without socks (yeah, it was straight serious today), I grabbed a pair of sunglasses to avert the sun. I kept these little walks with Hershey pretty quiet in the morning, not wanting to wake the house, and managed to keep things silent when I snuck outside.

The cold air hit like a bitch at first impact, but eventually, I got used to it, my boots scraping against the salted walk. Hershey and I took the trails behind the house, a pretty scenic park back there. It was easy to navigate with the signs, and since people did jog and walk back there, they kept the area clean and even cleared the snow from the trails for hikers. I didn't pass a lot of people considering how early Hershey and I went for walks, but when I did, I always moved for the occasional jogger. I tried to do that today as someone came up behind me, but as I heard the person slow down, I tugged Hershey's leash to a stop. I smelled the person before I saw them, and when I turned, my gaze filled with Royal Prinze.

Puffs of cold air came from full lips, his perfect cheek-bones filled with red color. His golden locks feathered in the chilly breeze, the boy jogging in place in a pair of too-tight jogging pants. Like seriously, they were two seconds away from being nylon leggings, lining his muscular legs like a second skin. Coming to a stop, he pulled an AirPod out of his ear, nothing but Under Armour covering his broad physique. He parted his lips. "Hey, Em."

Hey... Em. He said "hey" like he talked to me. Like we were even anything to each other anymore.

"Hi," I said, tugging Hershey back when she started to go over to him. She wanted to play, and despite keeping her away, he got to his knees with her.

"You've sure gotten big," he said, smiling a little when he scratched her behind the ears. He looked up at me. "She's gotten big."

I nodded, what he said fact. He played with her a little while before standing, taking out his other AirPod and shoving them both into his pocket with glove-lined hands.

"How have you been?" he asked me, tucking those big hands into the same pockets, and I could have slapped him. He asked me how I'd been, how I'd *been* like he hadn't put me through and *still* put me through hell on a day-to-day basis. He had to know how hard it was to see him with Mira. He had to know. He wasn't an idiot.

Or maybe he was.

"You're a joke, you know that?" I started to walk away, but hands and a body wouldn't let me. *His hands and his body* wouldn't let me, a chest touching my side, a curled finger and a thumb pinching my coat for me to stay.

"Em..." He breathed my name, his voice low and definitely not from someone who was at all virtually available. His tone wasn't mad either, which he'd clearly been that day he kicked me out of Windsor House.

I closed my eyes. "Don't. Don't do that to me."

"What?" He tugged me to face him, looking like he wanted to do more. "Don't what? Tell me."

Play these games and whatever the fuck he thought he was doing. *He'd* dumped *me*, abandoned me more than once and even my sister. He hadn't shown up for her at her service, consistent when he hadn't shown up for me either.

"You left me," I said, making his eyes close. "You left me, and you went with *her*."

Like he remembered that, he opened his eyes, his swallow hard. Immediately, he placed distance between, and I realized Hershey had wrapped us in her leash again. It was like she knew, knew what I wanted despite the feeling being incredibly stupid.

"I didn't want to," he admitted, then closed his eyes. "Leave you, I mean."

But he hadn't said he didn't want to be with her, Mira of all people. He didn't correct that. He hadn't at all.

He moved forward. "Things weren't a good time. I couldn't leave here..."

"So why didn't you just tell me that?" I gritted, all those emotions coming back. "I was alone. *I was alone*—"

"You weren't," he said, surprising me. "I knew where you were. I put you there, remember?"

I did remember, "put" someplace as he put it.

He dampened his lips. "That's why I had Knight check on you."

"Out of guilt?" I concluded. "Guilt because you didn't want to be with me? Because you didn't want to deal with everything that happened to my sister *with* me? Did you deal with it with her? Mira?"

"December—"

"Did you?" I got up in his face, trembling. "I saw you guys come to the reception together. Was that why you were late? Because of her?"

His hands came together, his lips closing and when his gaze averted I knew my answer. He had been with her, chose her for whatever reason beyond me.

"Things are more complicated than you think," he said. "Mira, she... I needed Mira."

He *needed* her, and why was that the worst thing he could have possibly said? Maybe because he didn't need me. Because she was able to give him something I couldn't, and for whatever reason, that enraged me. I think because I cared about this boy more than I wanted to ultimately admit. I more than cared.

I swallowed hard. "You needed her."

His nod was slow, his look pained. "I do, but I care about you—"

"Don't." I lifted my hands, not wanting to be some kind of damn consolation prize. "You can't have your cake and eat it too."

He cringed. "I don't want that."

"What do you want?"

"To not hurt you." He grabbed my hands, sharing the same words LJ had that day with me. LJ hadn't wanted to hurt me then either, all of this the dreadful truth. He squeezed. "To not hurt you in all this. My decisions. I loved your sister. She was my best friend, and I do care about you."

But he didn't have to love me, which he clearly didn't. He was between a rock and a hard place, wanting to not hurt me for the sake of my sister, but also not wanting me.

How fucked up.

I let go, done with all this. I started to go, but he called my name.

"I want you to stay away from Mallick, December," he said, causing my back to rise. He traveled close. "I know all this with us, but even outside of that, you need to put some distance between yourself and that guy. He's bad news. A bully."

A bully...

Were we talking about the same Ramses? The one who'd been nice to me while *he* left me high and dry for a chick who'd been nothing but cruel to me?

"You got some nerve." I faced him, face on fire. "Thinking

you have *any* say in who I hang out with. Ramses told me about that beef you two have. How you ruined his life because he crossed lanes with you and your little Court."

He smirked, no humor at all with it. He leaned forward. "Well, if I ruined his, it was penitence. He's not a good guy, and I seriously question his intentions when it comes to you. For all I know, he's getting close to you because he knows it'd piss me off."

"Fucking really?" I brought Hershey with me, my chest brushing his. "Not everything is about you."

"But sometimes it is," he said, pissing me off more. "And I'd hate for you to be caught in the crossfire because of that. Stay away from him, December. Seriously, he's not good for you."

"You're not good," I spat, making him swallow. "I just wish I would have known that sooner."

The swallow pushed hard down his throat the second time, and he gave himself away a little. I'd affected him, clearly.

His cheeks flooded more red. "Remember what I said. Don't do something stupid because you're mad at me."

He really thought everything was about him, and rather than give him the last word, I gave him mine.

I flipped him off through my mitten, his eyes on nothing but me. "Stay in your lane, Royal Prinze," I told him. "And I'll do whatever the hell I want."

Fuck if I let him tell me what to do. Fuck if I gave any more of my emotions to him at all.

CHAPTER
TWENTY-SIX

December

It was finals week and right before holiday break before I finally got to talk to Ramses one on one, the pair of us in the library studying for final exams. It'd been the first time I'd really been with him alone considering we always had people around us, and I really didn't want to put him on the spot about Royal's allegations. I may have been mad at Royal, but there were always two sides to every story. Ramses had the benefit of the doubt considering. Especially since we'd both been screwed over by one Royal Prinze. His head down, Ramses currently went to town on a mock test he graded for me, making way too many red marks on it for my liking. Turning it around, he slid it toward me with a single finger. He grinned. "Nice one, 'Zona."

Nice one?

"Seriously?" I swiped it up, all that red he'd placed on my exam *stars* not checks. I punched the air, then him. "I thought you were marking these wrong. What the hell!"

The librarian shushed me audibly. Lowering her glasses, she eyed the pair of us.

"Sorry," I mouthed, keeping my victory chant silent.

Ramses stacked his books. "Dare I say, you might be ready for this week?"

Yeah, because of him. I pushed my hand into my hair. "Oh my God. I might actually graduate."

"Well, you'd deserve it," he said, nodding. "You put in the work, so you're going to ace your tests. 'Gratz."

He held out his hand, and we did a silent fist bump. I'd apparently turned into one of the jocks because not only did I do that with him, but everyone now in our group. I grinned. "Thanks. I guess you are Dr. Brain."

He shrugged. "I guess I won't charge you—this time," he stated, chuckling that last bit. My smile faded a little as what he'd said sounded familiar to something else that had been said to me once upon a time. Royal once stated I didn't have to pay up for something, a favor between us.

How ironic who appeared to be his arch nemesis was putting the same work on me. Albeit in a different way. Ramses had never been one to act anything like Royal in the time I'd known him. In fact, I never would have believed he fit into this world at all back when we worked together in Arizona.

"What's up?" he asked. "You still worried? I think you'll seriously be okay this week, pass everything."

I shook my head, definitely not thinking about what he believed. I chewed my lip. "It's not that. Just thinking about something."

"What kind of something?" I had his attention now, his books back in his bag.

I shrugged. "It was something Royal said to me, something about you."

He zipped the bag shut, nodding. "Okay."

Here goes nothing.

I rolled my eyes. "He warned me to stay away from you. Well, basically beckoned me in the way he does. He didn't really go into specifics, but he said you weren't really a good guy. That you were bad news and a bully." There, I said it, all of it out there.

Ramses' lips closed, neither protesting nor agreeing.

I eyed him, kind of worried now. "Is that true? Any of it?"

"Possibly."

"Which part?"

He bunched thick curls, sighing a little. He'd taken his jacket off, really casual with his sleeves bunched up. "I suppose he's right."

"What? How so?"

"About the bully thing?" He shrugged a little. "I was a product of this place, I guess. Thought I was shit because I played a little ball and had a lot of friends. It also didn't help I was the mayor's kid, so yeah, I thought I was the shit. It happened, but I was eventually humbled the hell up when I lost everything, my friends, my rep, all of it when I crossed the Court. Turned out for the best, though, as far as I was concerned."

"Really?"

He nodded. "I was an asshole and needed to be taken down a peg. Probably made Prinze's life really 'fun' a time or two. Minor stuff, jostling him and giving him a hard time. Whatever. It is what it is, and I'm really not proud of it. I suppose he gave me my just desserts in the end, though."

"How?"

His eyes lifted. "You really don't want to hear about all that."

"Actually, I do. Actually, I *want* to know why you guys are at each other and what you could have possibly done to have him and all them raging at you." From what I knew, it really didn't take much with the Court boys, but Ramses had to have done something, *something* to make Royal come at me the way he did.

Long fingers drew down Ramses' jawline, thoughts behind his dark eyes. He definitely looked like he didn't want to tell me, but I had asked.

"I wouldn't do their haze," he said.

"Haze?" My eyes narrowed. "Like the stuff college guys do to get into fraternities? I thought that kind of stuff was banned."

"Well, this is high school," he stated, frowning. "And Maywood Heights. Anything here, as far as the Court, goes as long as no one talks about it apparently."

"What did they make you do? Or what did they try to make you do or whatever?"

He stared at me; long and hard, he stared at me. His jaw pierced skin as it worked. "I can't legally go into it. They make us sign NDAs just before, but let's just say, all those years of giving Royal a hard time caught up with me. He humbled me the fuck up, and I flat-out refused to do what he and the other Court guys were asking me to do in order to get in. It was nothing like what they had to do, swiping something from the corner store or streaking through a public park. It was crazy and I'd be crazy to do it, so I didn't."

"Wow."

His lips closed as he leaned on his arm. "Needless to say, people weren't happy. The Court's everything to these people. It gives you a lot of power, not just here but on the outside."

I knew that, had heard that. "So they blackballed you?"

"In so many words. I thought it was shit, and I let my dad know exactly what they wanted me to do." His tone changed, eyes almost sad. "He didn't stand up for me. Like I said, shipped me off."

And so here we were, Ramses against the Court world.

"Thank you for telling me," I said, honest about that.

"With Royal, it's like pulling teeth sometimes just to get him to tell me anything I want to know. I think he's got a lot of trust issues or something." In fact, I *knew* he did. Loyalty seemed to be a really big thing for him, something he called even me out on once before. I'd broken that trust with him, something he hadn't been happy about at all.

Ramses' look surprisingly shifted toward sympathetic. "He's not my favorite, but I know he's been through stuff. He lost half his family real young."

My ears perked up. "His mom and sister?" And when Ramses looked at me, I raised a shoulder. "I overheard him and his dad talking about it. Do you know what happened to them?"

"From what I remember, a car accident," he said, making my heart hurt. I really didn't want to care, but I couldn't help it. My heart did move for Royal, as much as I didn't want it to, and even if it didn't, anyone would deserve compassion if something like that happened to them. Ramses sighed. "It happened when we were in elementary school. Royal took it real hard, though. Out of school for what seemed like weeks, and when he came back he was real different."

"Different how?"

"It was like the guy couldn't see anything anymore. He was just a body, vacant, you know?"

I did. "I lost my mom young too. I get it."

His smile was sad. "I'm sorry to hear that, couldn't imagine and then your sister…"

He stopped as I eased away, sighing again.

His smile perked up. "Anyway, you're all set for this week, and to reward you for how awesome you're going to do on your final exams..." He paused, dipping his hand into his bag. He came out with an envelope, shiny and pearl-like with the finish. He grinned. "An invitation to the Mallick family's annual Christmas party. It's going to be awesome and snooty and snooty and awesome. My parents put it on every year. I used to be able to avoid it when I was in Arizona, but they're making me go since I'm technically home."

"I like how this is a reward for me," I teased, swiping the envelope. I opened it up. It had my name in elegant calligraphy and everything. "This looks like a big deal."

"I hate it, but it is," he said, his chuckle light. "Anyone who's anyone will be there, and it might be a little more bearable with you there."

I pushed the invitation back inside the envelope. "This is really nice of you. Like really nice, but this isn't like a date or anything, right?" I asked, making his brow jump. I gnawed my lip. "I mean, I'd love to go, but if this is a date..." I didn't really want to lead him on, not really feeling him like that.

Brown eyes lifted toward the fluorescents. "Relax, 'Zona. No offense, but I'm not really into you like that."

The words basically taken right out of my mouth, I shoved him. "Nice."

"Sorry." He raised his hands. "And it's nothing against you. I mean, you're a total bombshell and all, but I'm not really wanting to be tied down by anything this close to college. Anyway, everyone is invited to this thing. I gave Birdie and all them their invitations earlier today."

I got what he said about not wanting to be tied down before college and agreed, but I had to say, my cheeks did warm a little at being categorized as a "bombshell."

I opened the invite again. I guess I needed to figure out something to wear.

CHAPTER
TWENTY-SEVEN

December

Thanks to Ramses Mallick, aka Dr. Brain, I managed to pass my final exams without having to repeat the first half of my senior year. I wasn't out of the dark by any means. I'd studied to pass, not for comprehension, but as long as I did a little studying of my own over break, I could definitely be prepared for the second, and what would hopefully be the final half of my senior year. I was ready to go, get out of this place for good, and at least if I had my high school diploma, I'd have a fighting chance of doing something with my life once I put that school and this town in my rearview mirror. I had no intentions of staying like I had only a couple months ago, no reason now that Paige was gone.

This would be the first Christmas I spent without my sister, my first Christmas without virtually anyone. I wasn't going back to LA for the holidays. Though, I'd been invited. I spoke to Aunt C. whenever she could get me to answer, but despite her protests and damn near commands I'd come to her home, I wouldn't be. Rosanna saved me a place on her couch with her daughter coming home from break, and I decided to take it.

That didn't stop my aunt's Christmas presents from coming. She'd sent a couple, a few put under Rosanna's tree, filled with gifts for her kids and even some for me. I told Rosanna she hadn't had to do that, but she did anyway, and I'd gotten them all something too, grateful her family had allowed me to stay with them. She was cooking now, testing recipes for the day in question. I'd been on holiday break a few days and decided to give her a hand by walking down to the gas station and getting her some eggnog. I obviously wouldn't be drinking any of it, but since I was out of almond milk myself, my trek into the sleet and snow benefited both of us. I found it in the cooler next to the actual milks and nearly bumped into an officer reaching for a Gatorade on my way from the refrigerated section.

"Sorry, sir." The apology instinctual, I lifted my hands, then nearly dropped my plant milk when he lifted his hat a little.

He stopped too, round hat on and star badge glistening. The sheriff, the actual sheriff from my sister's... case stood in front of me.

And we both hadn't seen each other since that day.

My mouth went instantly dry, my gaze averting. I wanted out of here—now, but couldn't seem to make myself move. So much of that night had been a blur, but not this guy, his face burned into my memory. He'd been the one behind the glass with my dad most of the night before he'd taken Royal and the other boys away. He'd been the one who sent the worst news to be delivered to me outside of my mom dying. I'd been so young then, the doctors delivering it then.

Sheriff Ashford, a middle-aged man with a gray mustache, wet his lips. His fingers slid back and forth on the Gatorade in his hand, all this awkward for him too. "You're, uh, the Lindquist girl."

The one and only now, I nodded. "Yes... yes, sir. That's me."

He acknowledged that by taking his hat off his head, his swallow hard. "I didn't hear you were back in town."

He heard I'd been *out* of town, but then again, this moderately sized city was oh so small. Everyone knew everyone's business, and anyone who hadn't been living in a storm cellar for the past few months knew about me. I mean, how many people's sisters went missing only to turn up in the way she ultimately had?

My stomach sour, I swallowed hard. "Yes. I've been back a few weeks or so."

"Hmm," fell from his lips, his hand gripping his Gatorade. He put out his hat toward me. "I see you got some holiday stuff."

His reference to the eggnog, I lifted it. "Tradition for some people. I'm out getting it for a friend."

His grunt touched the air again, the hat bending under his hand. He really didn't want to be here. *I* really didn't want to be here. He cleared his throat. "I, uh, can imagine this season will be pretty hard for you. There's not a day that goes by where we don't think about your sister and what happened over at the station."

Get me the fuck out of here.

I blinked, swallowing once more. "Yes, sir, and I appreciate all you guys did. I'm sure that was hard."

"Not as hard as for you, I'm afraid." Another throat clear and his hat lowered to the side "I'm sure you have some good friends, though. The Prinze boy."

I frowned. "I do have good friends, yes," I said, not feeling the need to correct him. Royal had obviously been there and very vocal about wanting to know what was going on. So much so they'd guided him and the other boys away to discuss it in the sheriff's office. I found that odd then, that Royal and the others had so much power even there, but there was so much I didn't understand about this town. I suppose I never would. I'd be leaving soon, right after graduation.

Sheriff Ashford gripped his hat. "I'm sure it's hard for him too and the other boys. They were good friends with your sister and to all be there that night…"

"All of them, sir?"

He looked up at me, dampening his lips. "Yes. They said they were all there hanging out that night. Well, not the whole night. Royal said they'd all been called away by his dad, who also confirmed that. I suppose they all had some event to prepare for? Something to do with the Court? Anyway, they wished they could have done something, been able to prevent what happened to your sister in some way, which they couldn't have. Sometimes when people are troubled…"

"All due respect, sir," I said, my hand gripping my almond milk. "My sister wasn't troubled. She was a lot of things, but…"

"Of course," he stated, his look apologetic. "What your sister did after they left couldn't be helped was what I was trying to get at, and I apologize. Even still, the boys wished they could have. They cared about her."

I didn't know why, but I assumed it had just been Royal out there with my sister that night. I guess he never did say he was alone with her. I assumed.

Sheriff Ashford returned the hat to his head. "You take care now, you hear? Our thoughts are all with you."

I could gratefully breathe after Sheriff Ashford left, and after paying for my almond milk and the eggnog, I headed back into the storm, thinking about what the sheriff said. His version of the events had been different than I believed, but I guess I hadn't been really present that night. It'd been one of the worst of my life. By the time I returned to Rosanna's, I once again wanted to push that all back to the furthest crevices of my brain. I handed her the eggnog after getting off my boots and coat, and after putting my almond milk away, I curled up on the couch with Hershey and the TV. Rosanna's youngest were already in the living room on the floor, watching the Disney channel, and we watched together for a little while before Rosanna came out of the kitchen and pointed toward the Christmas tree.

"Your dad left you a package, December," she said. "I brought it home from work. It's a present. Nicely wrapped."

My sight panned to a new present there, the paper a ruby red and tied with the same ribbon. Rosanna's gaze on me, she clearly attempted to read me and my thoughts about said gift.

I didn't give her much, thanking her for bringing it over before going back to the television with Hershey and the kids.

"I know it's early," Rosanna said, frowning. "But I'm sure he wouldn't mind if you wanted to open it now?"

She was trying hard, wasn't she? Being the middleman when it wasn't her place. I appreciated everything Rosanna did for me, and I mean everything, but...

I forced a smile. "I'll go take a look at it in my room. I mean your daughter's room." Her daughter was out with friends tonight, so I actually would get to sleep in the bed tonight.

I said what I did to make Rosanna smile, and it worked when I picked the present up and headed to the bedroom. I didn't tell her about what I did once I got the box inside the room, and she wouldn't see it in the trash either.

I made sure it was buried deep in the can.

CHAPTER
TWENTY-EIGHT

December

"Damn, bitch. Who you trying to impress?"

The girls picked me up for Ramses' Christmas party outside of Rosanna's, Shakira's cool blue Hummer packed to the brim with not just basketball girls but boys. I recognized a few from our lunch table, along with some wrestlers.

I shook my head at what Birdie said, who was pretty much hanging out the window staring at me. I wore a nice dress tonight, red because we were on the cusp of Christmas. The annual Mallick bash was on Christmas Eve. I kept the outfit more my style with tall black boots and a leather jacket. Oh, and of course, my nose ring.

I smiled, taking the hand of a boy who offered me one to get in. Another took the trough of cookies Rosanna had given me to present to the mayor and his wife. She'd be staying at home with her kids tonight, off the hook, unlike me. It wasn't like I didn't want to go. I was happy to be invited and, of course, wanted to support Ramses. He'd been gracious enough to invite me, so yes, I appreciated that, but I just didn't have the Christmas spirit much these days. It was obvious the reason why, but I was putting my big girl panties on and dealing with things. I was here, and I'd try to be as happy as I could about that. If anything, because Ramses was my friend and I did want to support him.

"Shut up with that." I kicked the back of Birdie's seat with my boot for her insinuation, and she yelped with a laugh.

She turned, on her head a bunch of dark curls. "What?"

"You know what." She'd been doing that since she found out Ramses had been helping me with school. I explained we were completely platonic to each other *repeatedly*, but she continued to rag on me.

"Oh, she's just messing." Behind the wheel, Shakira wiggled her dark eyebrows, her dress a glittery white. Offsetting the umber color of her skin tone, the dress popped, and everyone was equally as festive in the back of the ride. I saw twinkling lights and even some Christmas sweaters, not gaudy enough to be considered "ugly" by any means. We were going to the mayor's house, and no one from my Richie Rich school was pulling one of those fashion faux pas apparently.

My chocolate chip cookies returned to me, I sat with them and did have to slap away a jock hand a time or two. They all could wait until we got to Ramses', the Hummer's mighty wheels crunching along the salt-covered streets. It hadn't snowed hard in over a week, so it was pretty clear.

"Fucking shit." The shock came from me, shifting in my seat as the road was literally filled with people and cars. We were at least half a block from Ramses' house, but the surrounding roads were already filled with people.

"Yes, girl," came from up front, Shakira. "Everybody's here tonight. I mean, everybody."

She wasn't lying, people already dancing in the streets as they walked up to the white palace ahead. I'd been there before, but I swear to God, Ramses' house battled the

Windsor House castle in its size. There were no other houses surrounding it. There couldn't be, not enough space with the football-sized lawn and expansive landscape. The white, column-adorned house in the center only acted as a focal piece, and Shakira pulled right up front.

"We'll use valet," Shakira proclaimed. "Ramses said it's more for the city officials and stuff, but he got us the hookup."

A man in a white jacket and bow tie sprinted out of a house constantly moving in and out with people. Shakira parked, and he came right up to our ride, letting us out. He gave hands to the girls and nodded to the boys, the girls and their escorts leaving while he took the car. I didn't have my own escort, but that was all good and well. I wasn't the only girl traveling solo tonight. From what I understood, Birdie and Shakira didn't have anyone either. We headed up to the door and started to knock before it opened right up.

"Welcome to the House of Mallick," Ramses exclaimed, his expansive arms wide. He wore an actual suit tonight, his tie a garnet red and on theme. It matched the pocket square near his lapel, the boy grinning like a man servant. "Come on in. My parents' home is your home."

God, he was such an idiot, and I told him as much as I passed him. I handed him the cookies. "From Rosanna."

He knew all about her, as did most of our friends as I mentioned where I was staying in the past. After I'd handed him the cookies, he looked up.

His grin widened. "You look very nice, 'Zona," he said, making me suddenly very aware of how I looked compared to him. He looked very nice too, shiny and like a brand-new penny. He looked like *money*, and since I never came from that, I almost felt awkward at the compliment. He saved me from having to respond when he analyzed the cookies. "And thanks for these. I'll give them to Lara."

I smacked him, my jaw dropped. Lara was definitely his

yippie French poodle he had inside there and he grinned again.

"I meant Francisca, our housekeeper," he corrected, waggling those busy dark eyebrows. He had his curls pretty managed tonight, a moussed halo on the top of his head. He widened the door for me and the group. "Come in. We'll see if we can find you all some floor space."

Our group descended onto the foyer, which was clustered the fuck up with people. Ramses hadn't been bluffing, people packed in the circular room. His family had a large Christmas tree, which greeted guests with its twinkling lights, presents lining around the whole presentation. I thought that might have been his family Christmas tree, but when he guided our group into the main event, aka his family's ballroom (because yes, he had one of those), that's where the biggest tree resided. It was seriously huge, suspended from the ceiling like a T-Rex's bones in a museum. Behind it was a small orchestra, a quartet with a conductor and everything.

And did I mention the snow? Yes, there was actual snow coming down from somewhere in the rafters. Not real snow mind you, just paper, but it softly coated the glistening stars in this very room. These people were stars, everyone in the room shimmering bright like diamonds in their luxury gowns and with their champagne flutes.

"Shit, Mallick," I stated, but I seemed to be the only one with a dropped jaw here. Everyone else laughed at what I said.

Ramses leaned in. "Can you tell my parents get pretty into this thing?"

Uh, "pretty into" was definitely an understatement. I idly wondered if Santa and his sleigh were going to come cruising in and asking me what I wanted for Christmas.

Ramses chuckled. "I'm going to go give these to Francisca. I'd put them on the food tables myself, but she's touchy about how she wants things."

At the mention of food, about half the guys went with him, the food tables on the far side of the room, and I saw them well. There was enough catering in this place to feed half the city, and I guess that was appropriate.

Half the city was literally here, and I immediately got dragged into a slow dance with my girlfriends. We danced in a bumbling circle, pretending we knew how to do the waltz or some shit. We weren't the only ones goofing and having a good time, though; other people from our school were doing the same. I was really starting to get into it before I saw some familiar faces.

"I guess everyone's here," I said, noticing Royal and Mira. He strode into the room with her, his suit fine and his blond hair pushed pristinely back. He still looked good. Still looked hot and was just as aware of it as Mira beside him. She did look good too, her dress a deeper shade of red than mine. Behind them both were other people from the Court, Jax, LJ, and Knight amongst them with their own dates. They all looked like a large pack of royals, extremely fitting.

"Nothing's going on with you and him, is there?" Birdie asked, pulling me in. "I know you guys had that hookup and everything."

I shrugged, twirling her. "Believe me, whatever that was is history." And gratefully so. I was done with the games and giving my heart to someone who clearly didn't want me. I wouldn't lie. All that with him still stung, but it wouldn't get any better if I continued to let myself constantly think about him.

Birdie's gaze lingered in that direction before facing me. "Probably for the best," she said, her smile a little stiff. I didn't know why, but in the next moment Shakira and Kiki came between us. They wanted to know if we'd like to join them for drinks, but since I didn't want one, I stayed put.

The three left me on the floor, and I did all I could not to watch as Royal and party mingled their way onto the floor too. I didn't have to stay there, so I ventured off, finding real estate by the big-ass Christmas tree.

Holy fuck. It's Dad.

My father had a drink cup in his hands, by himself and lingering toward the side of the dance floor. He looked a little lonely, and I forced myself from feeling anything about that as I watched him. He took another sip of whatever he had before a surprising guest came up to him.

Sheriff Ashford approached him, my dad stiffening. The sheriff must have surprised him or something, and looking around, Dad faced the man, the sheriff speaking to him. He let him for the most part, that was until the man placed a hand on his shoulder. Dad rubbed it off, looking *put off*, and before I knew it, he was falling back into the crowd. I almost felt compelled to follow him, but I didn't, of course. I didn't care.

"December, right?"

I turned, a beautiful woman before me, stunning. She had a spool of dark hair wound on top of her head, her dress a glistening gold on her curvy figure. She looked like a trophy wife and sparkled just as ethereal in the place. I also recognized her, quickly aware of what place I'd last seen her.

It'd been during the darkest day of my life.

She'd been at my sister's funeral. Birdie said she'd been the guidance counselor at their school for a time.

"Hi," I said, feeling kind of awkward. I didn't know her, but she looked at me like she knew me. In fact, her gaze bore over me like we were quite well acquainted.

"I never got to introduce myself during your sister's service," she started, but stopped. Her fingers tapping a crystal goblet, she seemed to be considering what to say. "I'm your sister's old guidance counselor, worked with her a bit her freshman year."

I figured as much, my sister with a whole mess of problems.

The woman moved her pretty jaw a little. "Anyway, I never got to say hi to you. My husband, Principal Hastings, and I left before the reception."

"Hi," I said again, and she smiled, oh so pretty. I normally didn't notice such things about people, but this woman seriously emanated. That said something in this place.

"She was very special, your sister," she said. "And I always hoped I'd get to say hello to you. She talked a lot about you."

My heart moved, melting its thick wall of ice I forcibly put up. "She did?"

I figured she hadn't. She hadn't spoken about this place to me, nor vice versa from what I understood. Birdie said she hadn't even heard of me when we originally became friends.

The woman started to nod, but stopped when her gaze took the crowd. I turned, but didn't see what she had.

"Anyway, I just wanted to say hello and make sure you got what I sent over. It was your sister's."

I turned, the woman pushing her pocketbook under her arm. "I'm sorry. You sent something over? To me?"

She frowned. "Yes, and did you not get it? It's a journal, something your sister worked in for a time. It's very private, and I don't normally give out students' things, but in this situation, I felt you might want it. I had your dad give it to you, sent it to his office. He promised he wouldn't open it, and I thanked him for that, valuing your sister's privacy."

I swallowed, thinking.

The package…

"I did get it," I told her, correcting myself. "Sorry, I'm just…" Freaking out.

My sister had a journal.

Knowing the thing currently sat in a trashcan, my heart beat to get away.

"You're fine," the woman said, her smile wide. She put out a hand. "And I'm Lena. I'm not practicing at the school anymore, but anytime you want to talk, about your sister or anything, that's fine."

I had been advised to seek out the guidance counselor in school, and though she wasn't there anymore, it wouldn't be bad to see her. I watched as she took out a card.

"My office," she said, handing me the card. She put a hand on mine. "I'm so glad we got to meet. It means a lot. I really cared about your sister."

Appreciating that, I nodded at her, listening as the music suddenly quieted and someone parted the sea of people. The man stood up near the band, his skin a softened golden brown, and the woman beside him a beautiful blond with thick hair that cascaded down the side of a powder-blue dress. She had her hand on his arm, and the man, I'd been told, was the mayor of Maywood Heights. He'd come to my sister's service.

Ramses' parents.

I looked at them, easily seeing a mash-up there. His dad was tall, and his mom was tall too, an Amazon like Birdie and the other female basketball players.

Mayor Mallick grinned. "I welcome you all to our annual Christmas party, and please, eat as much food as you can. We got to get our money's worth out of that bill."

The audience chuckled, my friends too, at least the ones I could see. Most of them stood toward the front, clapping after the mayor's joke. One person I didn't see was Ramses himself. In fact, I hadn't seen him since he'd taken the cookies. A quick rotation, and I noticed Royal, LJ, Jax, and Knight weren't around either, despite their dates being up front as well.

What's up with that?

The mayor said another joke, but I had other thoughts on my mind. I put my hand out to Lena. "Nice meeting you."

"Nice meeting you, December," she stated, her smile

warm. "I hope you get something out of the journal. I'm sure your sister would have wanted you to have it."

I would have, had it been the other way around, and thinking back on that, I excused myself for another reason. I hid on the other side of the big-ass tree, hunkering down to send a text.

Me: Hey, you didn't clear the garbage from the house recently, did you?

I sent this to Rosanna, waiting with bated breath. If I accidentally threw out my sister's journal...

She was taking too long, and since Ramses welcomed me the use of his house, I cut out of the ballroom to make a call. I hadn't been everywhere in his mansion, but I knew my way around enough to find someplace quiet. I passed attendants and caterers delivering more food to the festivities along the way and smiled at them all before dipping into the closest room I could find. That room ended up being an office, a fire softly burning on the hearth near a large oak desk.

I sat in the chair, swiveling around. I started to dial when a creak, then voices hit the room.

"You guys have taken to stalking people now?" came behind me. "And here I thought you boys were better than four against one."

Ramses.

I eased my chair around but just barely, peeking to the side of the high, brown leather chair. Four boys did stand against Ramses, and my heart jumped at the various sizes and builds. Jax, LJ, and Knight stood in a standoff with Ramses Mallick.

And at the center was Royal Prinze.

Royal had his hands braced on his biceps, his boys behind him like he was there to intimidate.

What the hell?

I started to move.

"Is this about December?"

I stopped, frozen by Ramses' words.

Ramses frowned. "She told me how you came to her, told her to stay away from me?" He shook his head. "Really, Prinze?"

"I thought she should be warned about who you are," he stated, easing his jacket open and moving hands to prop on his hips. "Or was I incorrect telling her what an asswipe you are?"

He really did have some nerve, but Ramses, I noticed, held no reaction but to face the floor.

He folded fingers over his face, a sigh on his lips. "Maybe you weren't wrong about who I used to be. I admit I threw my weight around here, but I'm past that now. All that's in the past for me, and it's not true now."

"It's not true now," Royal parroted, mocking him.

Ramses pulled in thick eyebrows. "Yeah, it's not true now, and anyway, isn't this all a bit much?" He put his hand out toward Jax, LJ, and Knight. "I mean, I get wanting to protect your friend's sister, but even this is overkill. What? You got a thing for her or something? Because seriously, dude, you can calm the fuck down about it. She and I are just friends—"

"We're not here about December," Royal growled, but could have fooled me. He passed a glance to the other guys. "Because if that's all this was about, believe me, it'd just be me and you standing here."

His threat lingered hard in the air, like it was warranted and he had any type of ownership over me and what I did. The audacity of this boy sickened me, and I nearly announced my presence if not for Ramses moving to speak again.

Ramses tilted his head. "What's this about, then? The need for the posse?"

"We represent all, bro," Jax intercepted, looking hard and not in his familiar ways. He was usually such a jokester, but his jaw clenched hard. "We represent the Court."

"The Court?" Ramses asked.

LJ nodded. "We wanted to make sure you knew where you stood…"

"And the place you fit in." Knight stepped forward. "You made a choice freshman year, and it wasn't Court."

Ramses actually chuckled more than I would dare to do in front of those mini tank trucks. He folded lanky arms. "You want me to stay away."

"What you choose to do is up to you," Royal stated, parting away from the other guys. "Just know it won't have anything to do with the Court. You keep on your side of the yard, and don't even think about going out and trying to join now, join us."

"Or what?" Ramses sneered. "No offense, guys, but I don't give a fuck about you and your shit."

"Let's hope it remains that way," Knight grunted. "Because even if you were in, you'll never be a part, not really."

"Nah, never," Jax finished for him. The guys all started to back away, all but Royal, that is. He remained firm in his position.

In fact, he gained on Ramses, getting in his face.

"You've been warned," Royal threatened again, looking the epitome of a mob boss. He turned away.

"I thought the Court was done with hazes out on Route 80."

The room seeped of all air, a vacuum sucking it dry to the point no one spoke. They barely even breathed, and I was amongst silence, my head shaking.

Route… 80?

"I thought you were done," Ramses continued, watching as the other guys came back. "Done after me."

The guys said nothing, *Royal* said nothing; meanwhile, I was having a mini breakdown. My sister had been out on Route 80, wandered the tracks before her ultimate death. She'd *died* out there.

Ramses' look could kill. "You know there can't be a more fucked-up way to make someone earn that little piece of metal on your fingers?" he stated, and my heart thudded into my neck. Ramses' nostrils flared. "I didn't do it. But did someone else?"

I bit down on my lip the same time Royal got Ramses by the shirt, the metallic taste of blood in my mouth. I shook, unable to see... unable to think. What he was saying wasn't true. What he was insinuating was bullshit. What he was...

Ramses didn't fight Royal, and I think that'd been the point. He wanted him to do something.

He wanted something to happen.

I shrank in the seat, seconds from throwing up right there. That's when a hand came around Royal's arm, LJ.

"Royal," he gritted, yanking him back. "Don't. Just don't."

Madness was in Royal Prinze's eyes, a madness I felt on the brink of traveling myself. The sheriff had said my sister hadn't been out there by herself, how the guys wished they could have done something.

"I'm sorry, December. I'm sorry..."

So many *sorry*s Royal had said to me that night, so many when they hadn't been his fault. My sister's death hadn't been his fault. At least, that's what I'd believed.

It took all I had in me not to cry out, biting down on my bloodied lip. If her being there had been because of them, because of this...

"Don't talk about things you know nothing about," Royal threatened again, but this time, his deep voice cracked. A clear emotion had been behind it, stuff he let go the moment he released Ramses. He pointed at him. "And you know what? You do need to stay away from December. Stay *the fuck far* away because if something happens to her, if you hurt her—"

"Something tells me I couldn't do worse than someone else," Ramses said, his swallow hard. He stood tall. "Go with your friends, Prinze. Go with your friends and leave my house."

Commanded. Royal was commanded, and I never thought he'd leave.

But he did, he did with all the guys, leaving Ramses, and I didn't get his response to that at all.

I fell, fell clear off the chair, and once I did, I cried my goddamn lungs out.

"December?" Hands came down to me, a tall boy in the room. Ramses Mallick was at my side, but the moment he got hands on my arms, I pulled back.

"Stay away. Stay the fuck away!"

"December—"

"It's not true. Tell me it's not fucking true." I hit his chest, blinded through tears. "Tell me they didn't haze my sister. Tell me they're not the reason she's dead!"

Ramses' mouth shut, his look pained, and I cried out more, his long reach coming around my shaking arms.

"I don't know, December," he said, rocking with me. "I don't know, but I suspected. That's why I asked Prinze. To see if I could get a reaction out of him."

And he gave him exactly what Ramses wanted. They all did.

"It's not true," I cried. "It's not. It can't be."

Ramses gripped me tight. "I hoped it wasn't. I knew what my haze was, and what happened to your sister was just too close. I didn't even put two and two together until I met you and started thinking about it. Once I found out who *you were* and your relation to your sister and hers to Prinze? It all just made sense."

"But why would they do that? *Why?* They loved my sister. *He* loved my sister—"

"I don't know." He looked at me, his face serious. "Maybe it was something else. Maybe your sister wanted to join the Court so bad she was willing to do something like that for acceptance. That was the one haze even our senior members directly forbade against because of me. There was so much of an uproar about it. I raised hell about it, and the Court wasn't allowed to do it again."

She wanted Court intervention…

Royal's words flooded back to me the night I found out about my sister, what she wanted that night and why she called him. Maybe that was what the Court intervention was, a haze.

A haze gone wrong.

I thought I'd be sick again, and standing, I attempted to leave.

"What are you doing?" Ramses was up with me, following me. He grabbed my arm. "Where are you going?"

"The police," I challenged. "There's not one word about this out there, about a haze or the Court being involved. They're saying my sister was drunk and wandered train tracks—"

"And maybe that's what happened." He grabbed me again, my arms. "Maybe your sister lost her nerve and she was leaving. The haze is they make you lie on the tracks. You make it through the night without leaving, you get a ring. Maybe she left. Like I said, lost her nerve—"

"But shouldn't the world know about that?" I asked, ripping my arms away.

Ramses frowned. "Why do you think they don't? Why do you think none of this is already out there? The Court and everything they do *own* this town. They control everything. Even the sheriff is in their pockets."

Chills, my body covered in them. The sickness rose again, and I placed hands on the desk to steady myself. I faced Ramses. "You think they covered this up? The Court?"

His swallow was hard. "I have no facts."

But I noticed he didn't say no. I sat in the chair, and lowering before me, Ramses got on his knees.

"I don't know what happened exactly out there that night, December," he admitted. "There's a lot of blanks, a lot of holes, but I think they need to be filled. *That's* why I came back."

I panned, finding his eyes. "What?"

He nodded. "What happened to me shouldn't have happened to anyone else. The Court has too much power, and they need to be stopped."

"And you're going to stop them?" I asked, shaking my head. "You lied to me, Ramses. Lied about why you were really here. You said you wanted them to see you."

"They will, and they'll see you too. They'll see *anyone* they've screwed over. Your sister deserves justice, December. You do too and me."

"How?" I cried again, a serious terror in my veins. I was so scared, so scared of the power and this town and even Ramses a little. I was scared of what he wanted to do.

And I was even more scared I wanted to join him.

"We get on their level," he explained. "Get in *their house*, and, December, I think with your help... We both just may be able to do it."

Thank you so much for checking out ILLUSIONS THAT MAY (Court High 2)! You can get the next book in the Court High saga, COURT KEPT, on Amazon.

Did you know there's a website dedicated to all things Court High? There is and it features exclusive content you can't get anywhere else! The website exclusives include playlists, graphics, character bios/photos, and so much more!

Want access to the website? Simply subscribe to my newsletter! There, you'll get new release news from me and a link to the newsletter exclusive Court High website. What are you waiting for? Get access today! =^)

Website access: https://bit.ly/3v7nTu5

Printed in the USA
CPSIA information can be obtained
at www.ICGtesting.com
LVHW021622160923
758255LV00031B/187

9 781958 046029